BUSHWACK BULLETS

Center Point
Large Print

Also by Walker A. Tompkins and available from
Center Point Large Print:

Deadhorse Express
The Phantom Sheriff

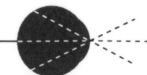

**This Large Print Book carries the
Seal of Approval of N.A.V.H.**

BUSHWACK BULLETS

Walker A. Tompkins

CENTER POINT LARGE PRINT
THORNDIKE, MAINE

This Center Point Large Print edition
is published in the year 2020 by arrangement with
Golden West Literary Agency.

Originally published in the US by Phoenix Press.

The text of this Large Print edition is unabridged.
In other aspects, this book may vary
from the original edition.
Printed in the United States of America
on permanent paper.
Set in 16-point Times New Roman type.

ISBN: 978-1-64358-508-6 (hardcover)
ISBN: 978-1-64358-512-3 (paperback)

The Library of Congress has cataloged this record under
Library of Congress Control Number: 2019952051

To
my dear beloved sister
Charlotte Edwina Tompkins

BUSHWACK BULLETS

1

THIRTEEN NOTCHES

DEV HEWETT twisted in saddle to trigger his six-gun at the rancher who was galloping relentlessly in pursuit. For five desperate miles the running gunplay had lasted, but Hewett's horse was winded and staggering so that the end could not be far off now.

George Siebert had caught the outlaw red-handed in the act of rustling unbranded calves from their Triangle S mothers. Hewett's idea was to haze the bawling critters onto Mexican range at a point where drought had nearly bridged the Rio Grande with sandbars.

Hewett had driven Siebert to cover with a rifle and then, boarding his ground-tied pony, had set out toward Mexitex in the hope of vanishing in the squalid Mexican section of the cow town where he had made his home.

But Siebert, sure of the justice of his cause, had pressed the chase hard.

On a fresh horse, the Triangle S boss was rapidly overtaking his owl-hoot quarry. Bullets whined with sinister regularity from Siebert's rifle. The Triangle S had been robbed for years by Dev Hewett, and now the outraged cowman intended to exact full revenge by finishing Hewett's outlaw career with lead.

Hewett's whiskery visage was gray with panic as he saw the rimrock of the Rio Grande looming before him. Mexitex town was around the bend, still a quarter mile beyond. Siebert was so close that Hewett could hear the clatter of the ranchman's horse; Siebert had booted his Winchester, had drawn a six-gun as he spurred in for the kill.

The big Colt in Siebert's hand roared, and Hewett screamed with horror as he felt the shock of the bullet hitting his horse. He instinctively kicked boots out of tapaderoed stirrups; an instant later his bronc crumpled in full gallop, and Hewett was catapulting into a dwarf smoketree on the brink of the Rio Grande's canyon.

George Siebert drew rein fifty feet away and swung out of saddle, hefting his smoking gun warily as he approached the sprawled figure of the cow thief. Hewett appeared to be dead, or else knocked out by his tumble.

"This'll save the county the price of hangin' you, Hewett," panted the stockman, holstering his gun as he saw no trace of life in the owlhooter propped grotesquely against the smoketree. "You've ambushed yore last—"

Even as he turned to go back to his horse,

Siebert heard Hewett's grunt of exertion as the outlaw bounced to his feet, the black bore of his Colt aimed at Siebert's back.

Siebert whirled, as Hewett's revolver spat flame and smoke and a heavy pellet of lead drilled the rancher's leg. Numb with bullet shock, Siebert still had the strength to ear back the hammer of his own gun.

Hewett was staggering backward in panic before the menace of Siebert's gun as it drove a tunneling bullet into his chest, ripping through his right lung.

Siebert collapsed in a faint, so that his eyes did not see the impact of his bullet carry Hewett backwards over the brink of the Rio Grande's high shale cut-bank.

Muddy water sheeted in all directions as Hewett's plummeting form struck a deep pool under the shale bank's beetling crest. A trio of Mexican kids clad only in ragged *pantalones*, were roused out of their drowsy torpor where they were angling for Rio catfish, a dozen feet from where Hewett vanished under geysering water.

Jabbering excitedly in Spanish, the *muchachos* plunged into the foamy waterhole and hauled the wounded outlaw to the muddy bank.

"It's Señor Hewett!" said one of them, staring in sickish amazement at the guttering blood which spouted with each heartbeat from Hewett's bullet-riddled chest. "The hombre who lives on the Avenida de los Palmas, in Mexitex—"

Coughing river water and crimson bubbles out of his lungs, Dev Hewett opened his eyes. A shudder of pain wracked the dying outlaw's body as he said to the trio of wide-eyed peon fisherboys who had rescued him from drowning:

"Go to the *abogado* . . . the lawyer—Russ Melrose . . . in town," gasped Hewett, the world spinning giddily about him. "Bring . . . Melrose here. He will . . . pay you . . . *mucho dinero*. Tell him . . . hurry—"

The largest of the three Mexican boys started off for the nearby town at a sprint, leaving his two companions petrified with horror near the stretched-out body of the outlaw. Russ Melrose was a well-known figure in Mexitex town, being the justice of the peace there; and it did not take the boy long to locate the lawyer, in his office above the grimy Purple Hawk Saloon.

The messenger boy showed no inclination to want to accompany the lawyer back to the fishing hole. And when Russ Melrose had worked his way through the dwarf willow and cottonwood to the spot where Dev Hewett lay, it was to find that the dying man had been deserted by the other two Mexican younkers. Hewett's groans and the sight of his ghastly bullet wound had been too much to watch.

12

"Dev!" cried Melrose, kneeling beside the gunman and peering about anxiously. "Who plugged you, Dev?"

Hewett's pain-shot eyes fluttered. His hand was limp in the lawyer's grasp.

"Listen to me, Melrose. I'm cashin' in fast, sabe? But before I go . . . want to get you . . . to do somethin' . . . for me."

With a shaking fist, Dev Hewett pulled a six-gun from its basket-woven holster at his left thigh. It was a gun that bore thirteen notches on its back strap—each a dead man—and Russ Melrose knew that Hewett was too proud to tally his guns for a common *mestizo* or Indian.

"Do you know . . . my kid—Everito?" asked Hewett, shoving the big .45 Colt into the lawyer's hand. "He's . . . just a whelp . . . three years old . . . now. You tell him . . . when he gets . . . to be twenty-one. Savvy, Russ?"

The lawyer nodded, staring at the gun in his hand.

"Tell him . . . it was George Siebert . . . who shot me," panted the outlaw. "Tell Everito . . . to avenge my death . . . by killin' Siebert . . . with this hog-leg. It's my . . . only legacy to him . . . savvy?"

Russ Melrose scowled thoughtfully. He knew that Dev Hewett had sired a half-breed son. Its Mexican mother had died in childbirth, and for the past three years the *niño* had been indifferently cared for by Hewett's second wife, Angelita.

"It'll take cash to support that kid for eighteen years!" pointed out Russ Melrose bluntly. "Then my fee—"

Rage and disgust made the blond outlaw flush in spite of the death-drain on his countenance.

"After all the years . . . we been pardners . . . in smugglin' . . . an' rustlin' . . . you talk o' money!" panted Hewett. A fit of coughing left him spent and gaunt. "While I lay . . . dyin' . . . you talk o' money. You greedy . . . shyster—"

Melrose stood up, a cold smile twisting his lips.

"Yeah—your sand is runnin' out fast, Dev. If you want me to hand over this six-gun legacy to your brat when he's twenty-one, you'll shell over a fee."

Dev Hewett propped himself up on one elbow. He pressed the palm of his other hand against the wound in his brisket, as if to stem the flow of lifeblood which drained his strength.

"All right. You'll get . . . your dinero," gagged the dying man. "Listen, Russ. I got . . . a secret. I found out . . . from a hotelkeeper down in Presidio . . . that a prospector named Warren Allen . . . has struck a gold mine out in the Sierra Secos."

Melrose scowled, his lips compressing thoughtfully.

"Allen is bringin' a map . . . to Mexitex . . . tonight. I was figgerin' . . . on waylayin' him . . .

14

myself. You salivate that prospector . . . an' you got a . . . gold mine, Russ. All I ask . . . in return . . . is that you give Everito . . . that six-gun . . . when the time comes—"

The expiring criminal lapsed off into another paroxysm.

Russ Melrose dropped to a squat beside Dev Hewett.

"Talk fast, Dev!" urged the callous-hearted lawyer. "Where can I find this prospector? Where's he got that gold map?"

Melrose had to put his ear close to Hewett's lip, so faint were the dying outlaw's whispered words:

"Allen's family . . . livin' in that covered wagon . . . west edge o' Mexitex by the river . . . behind the slag pile o' the copper mine. Allen's . . . comin' up from Presidio . . . today. You'll find him . . . visitin' his family . . . in that covered wagon. You—"

A ghastly rattle sounded in Hewett's windpipe.

"Yes—go on!" rasped Melrose. "What—"

He broke off, as he saw that Dev Hewett was a dead man.

The cow-town lawyer squatted for several minutes beside the twitching corpse of the Texas desperado. The circumstances of Dev Hewett's last gun fight with George Siebert, owner of the Triangle S spread, were unknown to Melrose.

15

All he had been able to gather, from the breathless Mexican stripling who had informed him of Hewett's whereabouts, was an impossible tale about Hewett's having dropped out of the sky into their fishing pool.

Three abandoned fishing poles nearby, and a string of catfish jerking feebly at the water's edge bore out the *muchacho*'s statement. And it was possible that Hewett had been shot on the brink of the low cliff overhead; or had Siebert hurled the outlaw's body in the Rio to hide it?

A crafty grin bent Melrose's lips as he pondered the setup which fate had shoved into his lap. There was a very good chance that he could pin a murder onto the wealthy Triangle S cattleman, and if so, nothing could please Melrose better. The unscrupulous lawyer had long had designing eyes on Siebert's range; it was the best watered and most level acreage in the entire Texas Big Bend country.

He put little stock in Hewett's fantastic tale of a prospector returning to town with a map showing where he had struck a gold mine out in the desolate Sierra Seco range. Nevertheless, it would be worth looking into. Hewett had died before explaining just how the Presidio hotel-keeper knew that this Warren Allen hombre was bound for Mexitex with the key to a golden treasure in his possession.

Glancing about to make sure his ghoulish

operations were not being witnessed from either side of the Rio Grande, Melrose explored the dead outlaw's pockets. He found nothing but water-sogged tobacco, a few *pesetas* in Mex change, and a bandanna.

The lawyer stood up, and thrust Hewett's cedar-butted Colt .45 six-gun into the pocket of his black frock coat.

Then he pushed his way back through the brambles to the riverbank trail which led to a bluff overlooking Mexitex town.

It was a nondescript assemblage of adobe-walled shacks, false-fronted saloons rimming a main street, and a copper mining plant which gave the town its excuse for existence. The curving Rio Grande bisected Mexitex, half of it on the Texas side, half of it in Chihuahua; bridged by a wooden-piled span with Federal immigration and customs headquarters at either end.

Mexitex was the seat of Yaqui County, and as such boasted a small courthouse—where Melrose had a justice's office—and a one-story adobe jailhouse in which Sheriff Les Kingman maintained the headquarters of law and order.

Thoughts were rapidly taking form in the lawyer's brain as he made his way toward the sheriff's office. Melrose was tall, angular, and bony; his face had the lean and predatory look of a callous undertaker, and his neck reminded men of a vulture's.

Among the better-class Americans, Russ Melrose was judged to be an unscrupulous shyster—a stigma which could have been based on fact had the citizens of Mexitex cared to check up on Melrose's past, when a murder and bribery charge had sent him hightailing out of an Alabama town ten years before, two hops ahead of an irate posse.

Out here on the remote Texas border, Russ Melrose shelved his Blackstones, rented a rolltop desk, and plunged into Yaqui County politics, hoping someday to corral the choice cattle range of the area and establish himself in the enviable position now occupied by George Siebert.

Melrose licked his lips excitedly as he discovered Sheriff Les Kingman seated at his desk in the jailhouse office. Kingman was a rawboned oldster who had seen careers as a Texas Ranger and a U. S. Marshal before settling down in Mexitex as sheriff.

Onion-bald, his skin dyed saddle-brown by the winds and suns of almost seventy summers, Kingman was a lawman of the old school who knew how to use his guns to enforce the authority of the tarnished star on his sombrero crown.

"I'm reporting a murder, Kingman," grunted Russ Melrose without preamble. "Some Mex buttons were fishin' on the Rio. They came and got me, told me that Dev Hewett—"

Les Kingman waved off the lawyer, swinging

in his chair to hook a booted leg over his spur-scuffed desk.

"I already know about that—sent a deputy over to pick up Hewett's carcass not five minutes ago," grunted the sheriff, waggling a toothpick under his sandy waterfall mustache.

"You—you know who murdered Dev?"

Kingman rubbed a horny knuckle along his stubbed jaw.

"It wasn't murder. George Siebert shot him after a runnin' gun fight. Hewett was chousin' Triangle S beef. It's a wonder that buscadero ain't been plugged long before this."

Melrose felt a rush of disappointment surge through him at the sheriff's cold dismissal of any murder guilt against Seibert.

"But . . . but Hewett said before he croaked that—that he was just riding across Triangle S range, and Siebert bushwacked him—"

The sheriff snorted his contempt.

"Hell, Siebert ain't a dry-gulcher, an' you know it, Russ. Besides, George has got two or three of his cowhands to witness the whole thing except the final shootout."

Kingman pointed through the open doorway toward a shack where the town medico, Doc Harry Hanson, had his home and county coroner's office.

"Siebert druv into town an' told me the whole thing," the sheriff said. "Siebert's got a smashed knee—Doc says he may never walk again. He's tryin' to fish out Hewett's slug over there now."

Russ Melrose grunted his disappointment at the turn of events, and made his way out of Kingman's office. For want of anything better to do, he presented his pass-card credentials at the port of entry gate, crossed the Rio Grande into the Mexican section, and looked up Hewett's shabby *jacal* on the Avenida de los Palmas.

There, he found that the Mexican fisherboys had already acquainted Hewett's Mexican wife, Angelita, of her husband's death.

Melrose found the slatternly Mexican *señora* busy gathering together her meager possessions, while on the dirty floor in the front room played Everito, the three-year-old half-breed child to whom Dev Hewett had bequeathed his notched six-gun.

"Si—I know that Dev is *muerte*," grunted the Mexican woman. "Me, I go to my padre's in Chihuahua. Do I take the *niño*? Do I take Everito with me? *Seguromente*, no. No caballero would marry Angelita eef she had a babee. What becomes of Everito, I no care, Señor Melrose. I do not love the keed. I am not his *madre*."

The scoundrelly lawyer could not repress a feeling of shock at the cold-hearted refusal of the peon woman to care for her orphaned stepchild. As Hewett's lawyer, he knew that indirectly he would be responsible for the heir's welfare.

"You are a bad woman, Angelita. Mexitex is better off without you."

As Melrose returned to the American side of town, his eyes ranged over to the westward, beyond the sluggish Rio Grande's bending channel. Just beyond the towering black slag dump of the Texas Queen Copper Co.'s plant, he made out a canvas-hooded prairie schooner drawn up under a giant cottonwood tree near the river's edge.

"Hewett wasn't spoofing any about a covered wagon being over there," grunted the lawyer to himself. "The least I can do is check up on his yarn about a gold prospector comin' here to visit his family tonight. If this Warren Allen hombre has a gold map, I'll damned soon know about it."

2

ALLEN'S GOLD CHART

SOON after the sun had settled into the distant notch which the Rio Grande had eroded out of the sky-line to westward, lawyer Russ Melrose made his way cautiously around the base of the man-made mountain of slag, his eyes peering at Allen's wagon.

A slim young woman was there, cooking over an open fire near the prairie schooner which was her home. A boy about three years of age was frolicking near the campfire, and Melrose recalled having seen this woman, with her son, walking along the streets of Mexitex.

"Her husband hasn't arrived yet," surmised Melrose. "Dev said he was due tonight. I reckon there's enough at stake for me to wait around a spell."

He could tell by Mrs. Allen's attitude of expectancy—her frequent glances toward the riverbank trail, and her general bearing—that she was awaiting someone's coming. Melrose did not have long to wait.

Even as twilight shadows were deepening, the

atmosphere seeming to press the campfire smoke close to the ground, a lone horseman appeared down the Rio Grande trail. The rider spurred his tired cayuse into a lope, and waved his sombrero in eager greeting as he flung himself from saddle and rushed to sweep his young son into his arms, then hug his wife close.

"We got your letter, dear," Melrose heard the woman say, when their first excited greetings were over. "I'm sorry we weren't in Presidio when you got there, but there was a smallpox epidemic raging—I thought I should come up here, where Hap would be safe."

Melrose felt his heart slam with excitement at Allen's words, which carried distinctly to where the lawyer was hiding:

"It was worth the extry ride, Eleanor. I've got great news. We won't have to worry about Hap gettin' his schoolin,' or bein' comfortable in our old age. Let's get in the wagon where it ain't so chilly, an' I'll tell you all about it."

Melrose stifled an oath of disappointment as he saw the Allens climb into the wagon. Their happy voices came from within; and a moment later Melrose saw their silhouetted shadows on the canvas, cast there by the lemon-yellow glow of a lamp.

Melrose drew in his breath huskily. He felt for the reassuring bulk of a shoulder-holstered Colt .45 under his frock coat lapel.

Then, glancing about through the gathering darkness to make sure no loitering Mexicans were about, he came out of hiding and slipped across the open ground toward the Allens' camp, making a wide circuit to avoid the pink glow of firelight.

He approached the prairie schooner from the river side, noiseless as a ghost as he passed the picketed horse of the Allen wagon.

Then, reaching the end gate of the Conestoga wagon, the lawyer cupped palm to ear and picked up Warren Allen's excited voice:

"One-eye an' me found some float ore in a dry arroyo, darlin'. That was three months ago, just after I left you folks down in Presidio. Well, we followed up that ore, findin' plenty o' yellow color in the gravel, an' a few nuggets. I got 'em here—"

Melrose risked a peep through the puckered oval-shaped opening which was in the rear of the wagon hood.

He saw Warren Allen and his wife bending over a buckskin poke as they sat on a blanketed bed. A tiny stream of nuggets flashed in the lamplight as the prospector poured the golden fragments into his wife's hand.

"And there's more where this came from, Warren?" The woman's voice was low-pitched with excitement.

The prospector kissed her.

"Plenty more, Eleanor. One-eye an' me found the vein that fed that arroyo a million years ago. It's a lucky strike, a bonanza, no less! After a lifetime o' grubbin' an' shovelin', honey, One-eye an' me are rich. Rich!"

Russ Melrose, forgetful that his twisted visage might be visible through the wagon-hood opening in case Allen or his wife chanced to look up, saw the happy couple bend over the wriggling and playful form of their child, to embrace ecstatically.

"Where is this . . . this strike, Warren?" the woman asked, finally. "Is it far from here?"

The prospector chuckled, and Russ Melrose ducked back out of sight, his ears straining to pick up every kernel of information that Allen might drop.

"It's took me six days to get here. It's out in the wildest, most inaccessible part of the Sierra Seco range. That's why that gold has lain there so long, Eleanor, without some other hardrock miner locatin' it."

Melrose could hear the heavy breathing of the prospector's wife. No doubt she had endured years of hardship, waiting for just this bit of news. Now it had come, and the realization that wealth lay before them was almost too much to realize.

"Is One-eye there now?" Eleanor Allen asked.

"No—we decided that One-eye would take the

pack string up to Fort Stockton to get supplies an' tools. We'll have to make a little stamp mill, sluice boxes an' stuff. Me, I decided to come back here, pronto, to get you an' Hap."

Eleanor Allen voiced the question which had leaped instantly to the mind of the eavesdropping lawyer outside the wagon:

"But Warren—if it's in such wild, trackless country as you say—what if you lose the location? You and One-eye might hunt the rest of your lifetimes and never locate it again."

Allen's booming chuckle reassured her.

"You won't have to worry, honey. Me an' One-eye thought of that. So we made a map. Only one copy, an' I got that with me. One-eye is to meet us at Marfa when he gets back from Fort Stockton. We'll use the map to follow our trail back into the Sierra Secos."

Once more Russ Melrose peered into the wagon. His face went hot with excitement as he saw Warren Allen reach into a hip pocket and draw forth a small sterling silver snuffbox. Opening the box, Allen revealed a small bit of soft sheepskin.

"Here's the map," Allen said. "It'll take us back to our mine, don't worry!"

Grimly, Russ Melrose shucked off his frock coat. From a pants pocket he drew forth a red bandanna, which he knotted over his face to form a mask.

Then, drawing his six-gun, the outlaw lawyer vaulted through the opening of the covered wagon's hood.

"Lift 'em, both of you!"

Warren Allen and his wife started violently, whirling about to stare at the crouched figure of the stranger who had leaped into their wagon. They saw death staring at them down the bore of Melrose's .45, saw a killer gleam smoldering in the slitted eyes between hat brim and bandanna mask.

With a hoarse bellow, the prospector stabbed a hand for a belted Colt.

Instantly, flame spat from the lawyer's gun and Warren Allen was slammed backward under the terrific impact of a bullet drilling his forehead between the eyes.

Eleanor Allen screamed, but it was not the hysteria of a cowardly woman. Eleanor Allen was raised in the outdoors, and now she was fighting for her life and the life of her baby.

Even as she snatched the gun from her dead husband's belt, Russ Melrose fired again, aiming through the spouting smoke clouds of his first shot.

The bullet caught the woman in the stomach, crumpling her with a sob of pain.

Behind her, little Hap Allen broke into frantic screams. But Russ Melrose disregarded the child's cries as he reached out to snatch up the silver snuffbox and the folded bit of sheepskin which it had contained.

Then, with a final glance over his shoulder, the lawyer blew out the lamp and crawled back outside. He snatched up his coat and fled through the darkness toward the slag dump.

Not until he was safe in the privacy of his own living quarters above the Purple Hawk Saloon did Melrose pause to examine his loot.

It was a gold map, all right. But, even as he looked at the waggly lines and mystic designs that had been drawn on the bit of sheepskin with a hot needle, Russ Melrose knew he had killed two human beings in vain, except for a few ounces of gold dust.

For the map gave no clue as to what section of the Sierra Secos the Allen gold mine was to be found in. It was a carefully drawn chart of a localized area, Russ Melrose knew it would be as hopeless as looking for the proverbial needle in a haystack.

Back in the covered wagon by the Rio Grande, Melrose had left a dead man, a dying woman, and a child. And indelibly etched in that child's brain was a horrifying picture of murder, a nightmarish vision of a red-masked killer that would sear Hap Allen's memory for as long as he lived.

3

ORPHANS OF THE BADLANDS

A mile east of Mexitex town, grizzled old Sheriff Les Kingman lived on his Flying K cattle outfit with Florence, his silvery-haired wife.

Tonight, for the first time in the fifty years of their married life, a child scampered about the Flying K ranchhouse, engaged in play with Wing Sing, their Chinese cook.

Every night for most of those fifty years, the lawman and his wife had sat down for a game of rummy—a routine which never was interrupted unless Kingman was out riding the range with a posse on some man-hunt trail.

"Rummy!" chuckled the sheriff, snatching up an ace which the old lady had just dropped on the discard pile. "Floss, I declare if you ain't losin' your memory. That's twice in this hand you've let me rummy a card on you. What's wrong, anyhow?"

The old lady smiled wistfully as he glanced over her shoulder at the sight of their oriental cook playing pick-a-back with a little tike that Sheriff Kingman had brought home to supper that night.

"I can't get my mind off little Everito Hewett, Dad," the sheriff's wife whispered. "What's to become of him, now that his ungrateful step-mother has run away to Chihuahua?"

The sheriff gave his wife a sidelong glance and rubbed his nose thoughtfully.

"I rattled my hocks all over the Mex section this afternoon, and none of 'em want Everito," admitted the lawman. "Seems like there would be room in some of those *casas* for one more little feller, but they all shrug their shoulders and say no. Can't say as I blame 'em—that worthless Angelita should have taken the kid with her, even if Everito ain't her own flesh and blood."

They watched the son of the slain outlaw, Dev Hewett, as he scampered about the room, his joyous laughter re-echoing through the home that for too long had been childless.

"Les," Mrs. Kingman said, polishing her spectacles energetically. "I never saw such a cute little feller, have you?"

The sheriff began shuffling the deck of cards indifferently, but his lowered lashes hid a peculiar twinkle in his eyes.

"That I haven't, Floss. Smart as a whip, and healthy as a bantam rooster. I reckon by the time he's ready for school he won't remember he got his start in a filthy Mexican hovel."

The kindly old woman nodded.

"And he favors his father's American blood

more than his mother's. He doesn't look like a *mestizo*."

"That's true. For a half-breed, his blond hair is plumb deceivin'."

Mrs. Kingman took a long breath and avoided the direct gaze of her husband.

"Dad, I've been wondering," she began tentatively. "Seein' as how Everito is so young—and seeing as how we always wanted children, but the good Lord denied us the blessing—and seeing as how Everito is an unwanted orphan, and all—"

"Yes, Floss?"

"I was just wondering, Dad, if maybe you and me—"

Before she could finish what she had started to say, a frenzied knocking at the front door interrupted her.

"Come in!" The sheriff bounced to his feet, hand going to a holstered gun at his thigh.

The door slammed open to reveal the Mexitex deputy sheriff, Bob Reynolds.

"There's been a killin' in town, Sheriff!" cried the lawman breathlessly. "Grab yore hat and come on."

The sheriff had a horse saddled and was galloping through the darkness with his deputy within five minutes. Even at seventy, Les Kingman was used to emergencies.

As they rode, Reynolds gave his superior what facts he knew about the killing that had sent him hell-for-leather out to Kingman's Flying K home.

"That woman who lived with her kid down in the covered wagon by the Rio—she come staggerin' up to the jail tonight. Covered with blood, and dyin' on her feet. She had her little tike with her."

"She wasn't dead when you left town to get me, Bob?"

The deputy lifted his voice above the drumming of hoofs:

"No, but her husband was. Dead as a tick in sheep dip. She said a masked gunman shot him and her while they was talkin' inside that wagon. Seems he's a prospector, name of Allen."

"Where's Mrs. Allen now?"

"She's fainted, and I lugged her over to Doc Hanson's. Then I goes down to the wagon, and finds her husband shot through the head. Then I lit a shuck to get you."

They drew to a bucking halt in front of Doc Hanson's lamp-lighted shack on the main street.

Racing inside, they found the medico kneeling at the bedside of a woman on whose face was the white pallor of approaching doom. She clung tightly to a frightened little boy who was standing at the bedside, eyes wide but tearless.

"No hope, Les," whispered the doctor, rising at the entrance of the two lawmen. "Bullet took her in the stomach and I can't probe for it. She's

34

wantin' to talk. Maybe she can give you a line on who did this."

Kingman knelt beside the dying woman and clasped his big gnarled hand over the one in which she gripped her child's chubby fist. A knot was in the sheriff's throat as he said:

"It's the sheriff, Mrs. Allen. Who done this?"

Eleanor Allen's eyes opened wide, and recognition gleamed in them. When she spoke, blood flecked the corners of her mouth.

"Sheriff . . . I want you to look out . . . for Hap. He's got an uncle . . . my husband's brother. His uncle's name . . . is One-eye Allen."

The sheriff nodded grimly.

"One-eye Allen," he repeated. "Can you tell me who did this shootin', Mrs. Allen?"

Desperation rose in the woman's eyes.

"Promise me . . . you'll see . . . that Hap finds his . . . uncle. One-eye can be located . . . over at . . . over in the town of M—"

A paroxysm of coughing seized Mrs. Allen, and she lapsed into merciful unconsciousness.

The sheriff stood up, turning to Dr. Hanson.

"If she comes to, find out where this One-eye Allen is, Harry," ordered Kingman. "Otherwise we won't know where to take this kid. Meanwhile, Reynolds and I will hunt for skunk sign down by that wagon where the shootin' occurred."

For the better part of an hour, the hawk-eyed

35

old sheriff hunted in vain for clues, in and around the ill-fated prairie schooner by the Rio's edge. But the slag-carpeted ground held no boot prints, and an exhaustive search by lantern light disclosed no discarded mask, no ejected cartridges, or any other clue that would shed light on the night's outrage.

After removing Warren Allen's stiffening corpse to the morgue in the rear of Hanson's shack, the sheriff entered the doctor's office to find that a sheet had been drawn over Mrs. Allen's still form.

The doctor had just finished mixing a sedative to bring sleep to Hap Allen, the stout-hearted little son who had been orphaned by the unknown slayer's bullets.

"She died without recoverin' consciousness, Sheriff," reported Dr. Hanson. "What's to become o' this child?"

Sheriff Les Kingman wagged his head sadly.

"I'll take him home tonight," decided the sheriff finally. "This is nasty business, Doc. It's too bad she didn't give us some line on what happened—before she went."

Back at his Flying K ranchhouse, Kingman found his wife still up. Everito, the orphaned son of a notorious thief, was sleeping soundly in a spare bedroom.

"Here's another little chap to keep Everito company, Mama," whispered the sheriff, placing the sleeping child into her arms. "You was aimin' to adopt Everito, wasn't you?"

With tears streaming down her aged cheeks, Florence Kingman nodded hopefully.

"It's O.K. by me, Mama," agreed the sheriff. "And if little Hap's uncle doesn't show up, I'll get lawyer Melrose to draw up legal adoption papers for the two kids. We'll give 'em our name, and they'll never know what was in their past, I reckon."

Mrs. Kingman smiled through the tears.

"I'm glad," she said. "It—it isn't proper for a child to grow up without a brother and play-mate."

4

AFTER EIGHTEEN YEARS

EIGHTEEN years brought their inevitable change to Yaqui County and its peoples.

Mexitex remained much as it had always been, a squalid border town with saloons outnumbering its stores; its shacks growing more weather-beaten with the years; and the Texas Queen Copper Co., having exhausted its resources, had gone into bankruptcy shortly after its slag dump had encroached upon and overflowed the spot of ground where Warren Allen's covered wagon had been camped by the river, erasing forever the stage set of tragedy.

The cemetery had doubled in size. Outlaws had gone to fill nameless boothill graves. Warren and Eleanor Allen slept side by side under one stone, but of late years weeds had overgrown the mounds and flowers were no longer kept blooming there.

The flowers had been Mrs. Kingman's idea, but Mrs. Kingman had died of a broken heart five years before, following the death of her husband. Game old Sheriff Kingman had died with his boots on, victim of a Mexican smuggler known as Señor Giboso.

Bob Reynolds, the deputy, now maintained Texas law and order in Mexitex. Murder cases were tried before a man who had graduated from a cow-town lawyer to a judgeship—Russ Melrose. And eighteen years had seen Melrose grow in power and wealth.

Melrose had lived to gain his ambition of being the power behind Yaqui County politics. He was the second largest range owner in the Big Bend country now—second only to George Siebert, whose Triangle S ranch had grown until it was incorporated under Texas law as the Mexitex Land & Cattle Syndicate.

Among the few small ranches which Russ Melrose had never been able to seize through tax sale or mortgage foreclosure—and a ranch which had not joined the ever-growing syndicate controlled by George Siebert—was the tiny Flying K outfit that had been owned by Sheriff and Mrs. Les Kingman.

Except for the fact that the Flying K range bordered the Rio Grande, and therefore had proximity to an inexhaustible water supply, Russ Melrose had never particularly coveted the sheriff's range.

Besides, Russ Melrose controlled the Flying K in fact, if not in title. For Melrose, as the only lawyer in Yaqui County, was the legal guardian of the young cowboys who had inherited the Kingman estate—cowboys who were known, locally, as the Kingman twins.

Hap and Everett, their names were; and identical enough in stature to be twins by bond of blood. Both had developed into six-foot specimens of manhood; both had gained proficiency in riding and roping, in handling guns and ponies.

There the resemblance ended.

Hap Kingman—so called from his happy disposition since infancy—had hair as black as a raven's wing, and eyes to match. His brother Everett had hair like sisal straw, and his eyes were cold and colorless, like chips of yellow agate.

Since the deaths of Sheriff Kingman and his wife, Hap had assumed the role of foreman on the small cattle outfit, going on trail drives as its rep, and in general handling the Flying K's business.

Everett, on the other hand, had chosen the companionship of saloon rowdies in Mexitex; he was more interested in courting sloe-eyed Mexican señoritas or developing his skill at roulette or poker, than he was in acquiring honest blisters from a lariat.

The morning of April 10th dawned clear and bright after a week of rains. The Texas sky was as blue as enamel, and the lifting sun promised the usual humid heat common to that section of the Rio Grande country in springtime.

The Rio Grande was no longer a sluggish series of puddles, but was swollen by freshets from El Paso to the Gulf. The added difficulty in crossing the river had helped the border patrol in their ceaseless vigilance against smugglers and border-hoppers.

"Reminds me of the morning of April 10th when Dev Hewett was shot to hell by George Siebert," thought Russ Melrose, arriving at his office in the Purple Hawk Saloon building. "Lots has happened since then. A lot of water over the dam—"

Picking his teeth with a gold toothpick, the cow-town judge stared off through the windows toward the tawny ridges which marked George Siebert's cattle range.

Dry season or no, Siebert's range was never in danger from a shortage of water; artesian wells protected him. His Triangle S range was always bountifully grassed, and syndicate herds fattened thereon.

Melrose turned to his desk. Beside it was a black steel vault, and Melrose was whistling tunelessly as he spun the dial to open the safe.

He took out his appointment book. The court docket was free; he would have the day to devote to private business.

"This is the day I been waiting for—for eighteen years," commented the lawyer out loud. "With a little jugglin' of my influence, maybe I can get hold of the Flying K ranch. That'd give me a foothold against Siebert's outfit."

Penciled on the appointment book was scrawled:

"Kingman twins come of age. Read them Mrs. Kingman's last testament."

Melrose chuckled grimly and glanced at a turnip-sized gold watch. The Kingman twins would be at his office shortly, but the lawyer saw no difficulties confronting him. After all, was he not the sole possessor of the legal secrets surrounding the pasts of his clients? Had he not drawn up their adoption papers after the lapse of a year had brought no trace of Hap's uncle, One-eye Allen? Had he not drawn up the sheriff's will?

Melrose turned once more to his safe. From a steel-doored inner compartment which had not been unlocked once in the past ten or twelve years, the lawyer drew forth two heavy envelopes.

One sagged under the weight of a Peacemaker model Colt six-gun of .45 caliber. The other contained a tarnished silver snuffbox with an imperishable parchment of sheepskin inside it.

Those seemingly unrelated objects held the secret of the strangely scrambled destinies of two human beings who had been orphaned on the same day, eighteen years before. And the key to that drama was held by Russ Melrose, their legal guardian. Mexitex residents had never known much about the circumstances of the two orphans adopted by the old sheriff, and had long since forgotten what little they did know.

Melrose heard boot heels slogging on the stairway outside his office, and he made haste to shove the two envelopes back into the safe and lock the inner door.

The lawyer was busy with papers on his desk when the steps ended at his door, and a moment later he was greeting the Kingman brothers, Hap and Everett.

"Come in, amigos. I reckon you know why you're here. This is yore twenty-first birthday, and the day I'm supposed to read you the terms of your mother's will."

The two men seated themselves opposite Melrose's desk. Everett, the blond brother, was obviously in a surly mood; his eyes were red-rimmed from a tequila bout in a Mexican saloon the night before, as a result of which he had lost a hundred dollars *oro Americano* in a poker game.

Hap, too, did not seem to be in good spirits, although his eyes were unbleared and his hands steady as he sat twisting his cream-colored Stetson in his lap. He dressed as befitted his cow-boy life—in chocolate-colored batwing chaps, crescent-pocketed rodeo shirt, kangaroo-leather boots. As was customary in Yaqui County, both brothers wore twin cartridge belts and guns.

44

Drawing a legal-looking document from his desk, Melrose adjusted a pair of pince-nez glasses on his beaklike nose, and intoned in his best judicial voice:

"I, Florence Marie Kingman, being of sound body and mind, do hereby bequeath my effects, real and personal, as follows, to wit: to my sons, Hap and Everett, equal shares in the ranch jointly owned by myself and their late father, Sheriff Lester A. Kingman; said ranch duly registered in the State Capital under the Flying K brand.

"To my trusted and respected employee, Wing Sing, in gratitude for his long years of service, I do bequeath—"

It was Hap Kingman who cut off the lawyer's reading with an impatient oath.

"It isn't right, Mr. Melrose. I shouldn't inherit any of that Flyin' K ranch. Everett, here is the blood heir of the Kingmans. But I'm not. I'm adopted."

The lawyer's eyebrows arched with astonishment. So far as he or anyone else had known, the Kingman "brothers" had no hint of their past, knew nothing of the circumstances of their adoption by the sheriff and his aged wife eighteen years before.

"You can tell Everett is their son, and I'm not!" went on Hap Kingman. "Look at his hair and eyes and complexion—he's a dead ringer for his father and mother. Look at me, Melrose. I'm as dark as a Mexican. Les Kingman—much as I loved him and respect his memory—wasn't my father. I got proof."

Melrose's gaze shifted to Everett. The dissipated-looking cowboy was staring at his fingers as they rolled a quirly.

"What do you mean, Hap?" demanded the lawyer warily. "What do you mean, you got proof that you're not legal heir to the Flyin' K along with Everett?"

Hap Kingman shifted uncomfortably in his chair, shooting a sidelong glance at Everett.

"Not meanin' any offense, Everett, but I've always known you and I wasn't real brothers. I admit I was raised as your brother—but in all fairness, you ought to get the controllin' interest in the Flyin' K spread."

Everett Kingman shrugged.

"Whether we're brothers, or not, is no skin off'n my nose," grunted the blond cowboy. "Go ahead an' read the will, shyster."

Melrose walked over to the window, apparently not hearing the insult directed at him. His eyes slitted wolfishly as he stared out across the rooftops toward the distant range which belonged to George Siebert's cattle syndicate—range

46

which Melrose would give his heart to possess.

Then he turned abruptly to face the two young men.

"Hap is right—he's only adopted, an orphan that the Kingmans felt sorry for," said the lawyer, "Everett, do me the favor of leaving me alone to talk with your—er—brother. What I got to say is sort of confidential, for Hap's ears alone."

Everett shrugged, and put on his Stetson.

" *'Sta bueno*," he grunted, pausing to light his cigarette. "Don't try to gyp me out o' what's comin' to me, though, Melrose. I got ways to protect my interests."

And he tapped his holstered .45 significantly, as he went out and shut the door.

5

MEMORIES OF MURDER

WHEN Everett had gone, Russ Melrose turned to the cowboy beside his desk.

"You say you've always known you aren't the real son of Les Kingman," prompted the lawyer, with an oily smirk. "Just what you got by way of proof?"

A bitter smile played on the cowboy's lips as he leaned across the desk, his voice vibrant and earnest:

"Mr. Melrose, all my life I've carried a memory of a man in a red mask. A man who shot my father, and shot my mother. Where it happened, or why, I don't know. But even though I must have been young—around three—I'll never forget how my mother led me by the hand through the darkness to a house somewhere or other. I never saw her again."

Melrose recovered his composure with difficulty. Sweat leaked from every pore on his predatory face.

"What else you remember, son?"

Hap Kingman turned away with a shrug.

49

"My mind can't fill in the gaps, Mr. Melrose. The Kingmans, God rest their souls, raised me like their own. I never once told them—even as a little tike in knee pants—that I knew I wasn't their own. But someday I'll find out who that red-masked killer was. And when I do—"

Melrose shuddered involuntarily as he saw the hot light in Hap Kingman's eyes.

"I've never killed a man," whispered the cowboy, "but when I find out who murdered my parents in cold blood—when I meet that man—I'll blast his soul to Hell, even if I swing for it."

Russ Melrose sat down with a thump, trembling as if stricken with ague. And then, through the mental turmoil within him, dawned an idea—a diabolical inspiration which, even for Melrose's warped and fertile brain, he knew was a masterpiece.

For eighteen years, Hap Kingman had nursed in the secrecy of his innermost heart a desire to avenge his father's murder. That desire had festered within Hap Kingman's heart, poisoning his mind, becoming the one goal in life which he was bent on achieving.

Russ Melrose stood up and went around the table to drop a paternal hand on the cowboy's slumped shoulder.

"Hap, my boy, I thought I'd never tell you the secret of your past," he whispered hoarsely. "I even promised your foster-father, Les Kingman,

I'd never breathe a word of what I know to you. But—seeing as how you remember back to that night when your real folks was killed—damned if I'm not tempted to break my promise to the sheriff."

Hap Kingman leaped to his feet, a fierce light blazing in his eyes.

"You mean you . . . you know who . . . killed my folks, Melrose?"

In spite of himself, the lawyer shuddered at the ferocity in the cowboy's voice. To compose his own nerves, Melrose went over to his safe, opened it, and drew forth the heavy envelope containing Dev Hewett's notched six-gun.

He removed the Colt from the envelope and laid it on the big blotter before him. Rust had flecked the blued steel barrel of the Peacemaker, tarnished the thirteen notches on the backstrap. But the well-oiled weapon was still in perfect working order, still held the empty shells in its cylinder as a grim reminder of Dev Hewett's shootout of a generation before.

"I was beside your father when he died, Hap—and I got his last words," said the lawyer in a cold voice. "He told me who shot him—who shot your mother. Your father's name was Dev Hewett."

Hap Kingman was staring into Melrose's eyes, forcing the lawyer to keep his gaze riveted to the gun on the desk before him.

"You won't believe me when I tell you who

51

killed your folks, son. He's . . . he's one of the biggest men in Texas. One of the biggest men around Mexitex today. But he wasn't so big when he murdered your father and mother for what dinero they had—the dinero that gave him his start toward success."

Sweat was dripping from the point of Hap Kingman's jaw as he waited in agonizing suspense for Melrose to go on.

"Tell me," snarled the cowboy harshly, "who was it?"

Melrose rubbed perspiration from his buzzard-like neck.

"The hombre who killed your folks . . . was George Siebert. The hombre who now owns the Triangle S beef syndicate, Hap."

There was a long silence, a silence that congealed the atmosphere of the stuffy office and put a film of ice in Melrose's veins. When young Kingman finally spoke, it was in a voice like a knell of doom.

"If Siebert did that, why wasn't he hung?"

Melrose shrugged eloquently.

"It was only the word of a dying man against his. I told the sheriff what Dev Hewett told me before he died. But that wasn't proof enough to hang Siebert, who probably had an alibi anyhow. All I know is that your father put a bullet into Siebert's leg—a bullet that crippled Siebert for life."

Hap muttered a low, passionate oath.

"My father's word is good enough for me," he whispered finally. "Siebert's rich. Arrogant. A range hog. A cattle baron, they call him. And he founded the syndicate on dinero he killed two innocent people to get—"

The cowboy broke off to point at the six-gun on the desk.

"Why'd you take that smokepole out of your safe, Melrose?"

The lawyer's eyes snapped with guile.

"I was coming to that, son. Just before your father died, he whispered to me and said, *'Melrose, when my son Hap is a grown man—give him this gun. Tell him to avenge my death. Tell him to kill George Siebert with this gun—it's my only legacy left to give him.'* And then your father died."

With an impulsive gesture, Hap Kingman reached for the six-gun, saw Melrose snatch it away.

"You can have this Colt," rasped the judge, "only on one condition—that you won't ambush George Siebert. That will give Siebert an even chance to come clean and confess. Otherwise I'd be a party to Siebert's murder, Hap. Me being an honest citizen, and a judge to boot—that would be unthinkable."

Hap Kingman swallowed hard, then nodded. He removed a Colt from one of his own holsters, and when Melrose handed him the notch-butted gun, thrust the weapon into the scabbard.

"I'll give Siebert more than an even break. He can have his cutter out of leather before I start my draw, Melrose. And don't worry about whatever happens. I'll skip the country as soon as I've carried out my father's dyin' request."

Melrose, trembling despite his efforts to control his shaking nerves, accompanied Hap Kingman to the door of his office. There, the cowboy shot out a hand to grip the lawyer's.

"I'll never forget this favor, Judge Melrose!" said the cowboy. "Never. *Dev Hewett.* Why, I'd never even known dad's name!"

The lawyer nodded soberly.

"Forget it, Hap, and *adios* to you. I just hope— well, I know that your foster-father, the old sheriff, would have done the same thing if he'd known what I know about the murder of your real dad."

As Hap turned to go, the lawyer husked out anxiously:

"Don't give Siebert a chance to back-shoot you, kid. Siebert's a slick snake, you know. He wouldn't give you any more of a chance than he give your dad and mother."

Hap Kingman grinned crookedly.

"Don't worry," he said. "George Siebert's name is as good as written on a boothill tombstone this minute. I've waited too long for this chance at revenge, to muff it now it's come."

Russ Melrose shut the door on Hap's exit and made his way to the window, rubbing his palms together in an ecstasy of satisfaction.

"With George Siebert out of the picture, I stand to control that syndicate of his," chuckled the lawyer greedily. "Then nothing can stop me from bein' the biggest man in Yaqui County. Mebbe even, someday, the Governor of Texas."

6

"I'M DEV HEWETT'S SON!"

LEAVING Mexitex, Hap Kingman rode along the riverbank to the Flying K ranch where he had spent his adolescent years. His interview with Russ Melrose had cleared his heart of a burden that had been there ever since that death-hounded night eighteen years before. And he knew he could not wipe out the memory of his parents' murder except with gunsmoke.

He paused at the ranchhouse long enough to attend to the grim business of oiling his six-gun, the gun that was his father's dying legacy. He replaced the empty chambers with fresh cartridges, and fired a test shot at an adobe, bunkhouse wall, to get an idea of the trigger pull.

The thirteen notches on the backstrap of the butt puzzled him somewhat. Notches denoted a killer's gun, and it was hard for him to believe that his father had been a killer. But killer or not, the enormity of George Siebert's crime justified what Hap Kingman was about to do.

Saddling up the prize horse of his cavvy—a leggy chestnut saddler that Mother Kingman had given to him shortly before her death—Hap Kingman rode grimly eastward, making in the direction of George Siebert's sprawling ranch-house midway down the slope of Manzanita Hill.

He knew George Siebert by sight; but Siebert, his leg maimed by an old gunshot wound, seldom left the ranch from which he directed the far-flung enterprises of the Mexitex Land & Cattle Syndicate.

He remembered that Sheriff Kingman had always held Siebert in high regard, despite Siebert's testiness and grouchy disposition. But that deference was due Siebert's position as chief taxpayer and most powerful cattleman in the county, Hap decided bitterly. Even Les Kingman had to toady some, in the game of politics.

A torrential rain had lashed Yaqui County the day before, turning the tree-lined lane leading up Manzanita Hill to a morass of adobe mud. The rain likewise freshened up the foliage and made the white walls of Siebert's Spanish-style stucco home gleam vividly in the sunshine.

All of this wealth, Hap realized with a curse of rage, had its foundation on money which Siebert had murdered his parents to obtain. The flames of a long pent-up hatred burned bright within the cowboy as he flung himself out of saddle in front of the tile-roofed ranchhouse.

"Siebert won't take that wealth to Hell with him today," panted the cowboy, sloshing through ankle-deep mud toward the gate entering the fenced-off yard in front of the Triangle S house.

He nearly collided with a chestnut-haired girl who, dressed in whipcord riding breeches and an orange-colored silk blouse, was walking out of the gate, a quirt swinging from one wrist.

"Uh—beg pardon," gruffed the cowboy automatically, stepping to one side. "Uh—you're Anna Siebert, aren't you?"

Kingman was looking down into a pair of dancing blue eyes. He had seen the rancher's daughter once before, at a schoolhouse dance; but for the greater part of her lifetime Anna Siebert had been away at an expensive school in San Antone.

"Yes," she replied, in a voice that reminded Hap Kingman of mission bells he had heard twinkling in the distance. "You're one of the Kingman twins, aren't you? I met you at a fiesta once—"

She broke off, at the scowl which darkened the puncher's face.

"Reckon I am. Is your father home?"

The girl bit a carmine lip, worried by his grim tone. The cowboy was not drunk, that was obvious. Then she answered. "Yes. You'll find him on the porch on the north side of the house. There . . . there nothing wrong here, is there, Mr. Kingman?"

Hap pushed by the girl impatiently, making

59

his way toward the arch-pillared porch which flanked the long end of the house.

Anna Siebert paused a moment at the gate, then turned and made her way back to the house, entering by the front door.

Grimly, Hap Kingman stalked to the north end of the house and turned the corner. There he halted, legs spread wide, to stare at the white-haired old rancher who sat in a wheelchair in the shade of the porch.

George Siebert lifted a hand in greeting as he recognized the steely-eyed young cowpuncher before him.

"Drag up a chair and set. What's on your mind, Kingman?"

Young Kingman hooked thumbs in shell belts, his eyes burning into the syndicate owner's. When he spoke, his voice was as harsh as clanking sword blades.

"My name isn't Kingman."

George Siebert adjusted his crippled leg in the wheelchair and grinned patiently.

"O.K., it isn't Kingman. What is it, then? What's agitatin' you, son?"

Inhaling deeply, Hap snarled out with a voice that shook with the long-repressed hatred that had festered like a canker in his heart:

"*I'm Dev Hewett's son,* Siebert. Remember him?"

The veteran stockman jerked erect, his brows

gathering in recollection. Then he relaxed, his eyes sweeping up and down Hap Kingman's frame. His voice did not hint of malice as he said:

"I don't reckon I'll ever forget Dev Hewett, son. Dev Hewett's bullet smashed my kneecap and put me in this wheelchair goin' on eighteen years, now."

Siebert cocked his head, eyeing Hap Kingman with newborn interest.

"I knew Dev Hewett had a whelp," he went on, without rancor. "So you—Hap Kingman—are he. It don't seem possible. But then my friend the sheriff had what it took to raise a kid into a man like you, I reckon. He got you young enough, and he—"

Siebert broke off as he saw Hap Kingman break his trance, then step forward to thrust one of his Colt .45s into Siebert's lap. Stepping back, Hap Kingman snarled in a raw undertone:

"I've come to kill you, Siebert."

"Because I killed Dev?"

"That's right. This gun in my holster is the gun Dev Hewett shot you with, Siebert. I'm givin' you my other gun—and I'm givin' you to the count of five to start foggin' it *muy pronto*."

No trace of alarm crossed the old man's face.

"You've been drinking, Hap," he said softly. "Why should you bait me into a gun fight—on account of a quarrel I might have had with your father eighteen years ago? I hold no ill will for you, Hap. As for your father, he deserved—"

With a choked cry, Hap Kingman snapped his six-gun legacy from holster, fingers coiled about a stock that had thirteen death-notches on its metal backstrap.

"Use that gun, Siebert!" the cowboy screamed berserkly. "Fill your hand—"

The sharp explosion of a gun broke off the cowboy's outburst, a gunshot that seemed to come from near at hand and from a great distance, at the same time.

Even as Hap Kingman stared at the cattleman seated on the wheelchair before him, he saw a crimson rose blossom over George Siebert's heart, saw blood spread and gush over the white linen of Siebert's shirt front.

Then, his eyes glazed with death, the boss of the Mexitex Syndicate toppled limply forward to thud at Hap Kingman's feet, the cowboy's .45 six-gun clattering from his lap as he fell.

Numb with horror, Hap Kingman swung his gaze around to find the source of the mysterious shot that had felled Siebert before his very eyes.

Then a clatter of boots and a chime of spur rowels behind him made Hap Kingman spin about, to face Anna Siebert, daughter of the slain rancher.

The girl's eyes widened in horror as she stared at her father's corpse.

Then, lifting her shot-loaded quirt, she sprang at the stunned cowboy with a single word screaming from her lips:

"Murderer!"

7

HAP HIRES A LAWYER

HAP KINGMAN saw the shot-loaded end of the quirt zipping at his head, sensed the power in Anna Siebert's arm as she gripped the tiny whip by its rawhide lashes and aimed it like a blackjack at his temple.

But the incomprehensible murder of George Siebert a few clock-ticks back had left Kingman incapable of co-ordinating his muscles to defend himself.

The blow fell, with the *thwacking* sound of steel shot against bone.

Like a candle snuffed out in a gale, the cowboy's senses left him. He plunged into a swirling vortex of fire, then skidded into a black abyss of oblivion.

He was not conscious of Anna Siebert's scream, which brought startled Triangle S cowpunchers racing from barn and bunkhouse.

His numbed ears did not register the shouts and curses of the syndicate riders, as they saw George Siebert's crumpled body, with the girl bending over the corpse, fighting back the tears.

Even the hoarse yells of "String the devil up!" made no impression on Kingman's brain. He was out, cold. Blood dripped slowly from a raw welt over his temple, where Anna Siebert's quirt handle had thudded home.

"No, boys!" whispered the heiress of the Triangle S ranch, as she saw irate cowhands seize the limp body of the insensible man, saw her foreman deftly fashioning a five-roll handyman's knot out of a lariat. "No. We'll take him to town, and hang him legally. We . . . we can't have a lynching bee on the Triangle S. Even . . . even daddy wouldn't want that."

And so Hap Kingman was hustled into a jouncing buckboard and driven to Mexitex town, and the news of George Siebert's murder was soon being discussed over every poker table and whiskey glass on both sides of the Rio.

It was a full hour after he had been lodged in Sheriff Bob Reynolds' calaboose that Hap Kingman's brain began to flicker back to consciousness.

For a long hour he lay in a tossing stupor, fireworks dazzling his optic nerve, his pulse booming like a bass drum somewhere inside him.

He was dimly aware of the hoary-headed old medico, Doc Harry Hanson, visiting the cell and bandaging his bruised skull.

After the doctor had left, the jail keys jangled outside his cell again and Hap Kingman opened his eyes to see the vulture-necked figure of the lawyer and judge, Russ Melrose.

Melrose seated himself on the jail cot beside the prisoner and laid a gnarled, blue-veined hand on the cowboy's knee.

"What happened, son?" whispered the lawyer. "It isn't hard for me to guess that things went loco over at the Triangle S after you killed Siebert. How come you didn't make your getaway?"

Hap Kingman shook his head dazedly.

"I don't know. The girl . . . standing there. Conked me colder'n a catfish. That's all I know."

Melrose made a clucking sound with his tongue.

"Don't worry, Hap. I don't reckon a jury will hang you for killing Siebert, not when they hear what I got to tell 'em. Maybe we can plead insanity and get you off with a life sentence in the penitentiary. *Quien sabe?*"

Hap Kingman sat with his head in his hands for many minutes, collecting his scattered wits.

Suddenly he looked up, to stare at the lawyer.

"Melrose, I didn't kill Siebert!"

The lawyer closed one eyelid in a knowing wink.

"We can't make that plea stick, son. After all, Anna Siebert witnessed that mu—that killin'. We wouldn't have the chance of a snowball in hell if you plead not guilty. Perty girls have a way of swinging juries—even when the defendant is innocent. Which you're not."

Hap Kingman got shakily to his feet and commenced pacing tiger-like up and down the narrow confines of his cell.

"Russ, this may sound loco as an opium dream, but it's God's truth. *I didn't kill Siebert!*"

Melrose took a cheroot from his vest pocket and lighted it.

"That *is* remarkable—coming from you, Hap. Didn't you ride out to the Triangle S with the avowed intention of killing Siebert?"

Kingman nodded desperately.

"Yes. I handed him a gun, told him to use it. I gave him an even chance to blow me wide open, Melrose."

"But you beat him to the draw?"

Dismay swirled in Hap Kingman's brain as he struggled to piece together the hazy fragments of his memory, the events which transpired immediately prior to Anna Siebert's knocking him out with a quirt handle.

"I didn't shoot. Someone else shot Siebert. I didn't get a chance to fire that gun my dad left me eighteen years ago."

Melrose shook his head stubbornly.

"I saw the gun, Hap," whispered the lawyer. "Sheriff Reynolds just got through showin' it to me. He's holdin' the gun for evidence. It's got a fired shell under the hammer."

Kingman's jaw dropped, and then he remembered.

"I loaded the gun, and fired one shot to see how the trigger handled. But that was back at the Flyin' K. That shell wasn't the one that killed Siebert."

Russ Melrose regarded the prisoner through pluming clouds of cheroot smoke. He did his best to hide the gleam of satisfaction which smoldered in his pale eyes. He replied:

"Why do you keep insisting that you didn't shoot Siebert? Somebody did. At point-blank range. His body's over at Doc Hanson's morgue right now, with a bullet hole in his ribs you could poke a stirrup through."

In desperation, Hap Kingman struggled for an explanation. And then, in a flash of inspiration, a possibility struck him.

"Listen, Melrose. I heard the shot that killed Siebert; it came from a distance. What would prevent somebody hidin' in the chaparral up on top of Manzanita Hill, and pluggin' Siebert?"

Melrose grinned skeptically.

"That yarn wouldn't hold water with a jury, son."

Kingman continued pacing up and down the cell, a growing suspicion taking root in his brain.

"It had to be that. Manzanita Hill overlooks the porch of the Triangle S ranchhouse where Siebert was sittin'. Somebody hid up there, and ambushed Siebert. That accounts for the sound of the shot comin' from somewhere else."

Russ Melrose stood up, adjusting his coat lapels preparatory to leaving the jail.

"That explanation might hold water if the murder wasn't witnessed by George's daughter, Hap."

"It's got to be true, Melrose. I can't prove it, but it's got to be true. There's no other way it could have happened."

"Are you sorry," asked the lawyer, "that Siebert is dead?"

A lifelong torrent of anger mottled Kingman's face with color.

"Not by a damned sight. But I hate to stretch hang rope for a murder I didn't commit, that's all."

A deputy sheriff came at Melrose's call and unlocked the cell. Peering at Kingman through the bars, the lawyer said:

"I won't be sitting on the judge's bench when your case comes to trial, Hap. I'll have to be one of the witnesses, seeing as how I know you were threatening Siebert's life. They'll call in a judge from Del Rio to try the case."

Hap Kingman stared at the cadaverous attorney, a numb despair beginning to jell his heart.

"However," continued Melrose, "if you like, I'll take you on as a client. I'll be your defense counsel. It's up to you."

The cowboy spread his hands in a gesture of despair.

"I know I haven't a chance of beatin' the

gallows, Melrose. But if you think I got a chance, you be my lawyer."

Russ Melrose nodded, turned on his heel, and accompanied the deputy sheriff out of the cell block.

The Yaqui County courthouse in Mexitex was jammed to capacity three days later when Hap Kingman's murder trial opened. Cattlemen from outlying ranches, including the full personnel of George Siebert's syndicate; bartenders and gamblers, storekeepers and miners from surrounding mountain country all joined the welter of humanity inside the stuffy courtroom.

Amos Peddicord, a potbellied judge from the neighboring city of Del Rio, brought the courtroom to order. The first day was spent in the monotonous selection of a jury to try the case, Lawyer Russ Melrose stubbornly objecting to most of the men called on grounds that they were prejudiced.

Hap Kingman's friends were legion. The entire range seemed stupefied by the news of Siebert's murder, and there was outspoken comment to the effect that, for some reason or other, Hap had been framed. It was not compatible with the likable cowboy's character that, for no motive at all, he could have ridden out to the Triangle S on a mission of death.

Finally a jury composed of twelve supposedly

disinterested cattlemen and Mexitex citizens had been sworn in, and the second day of the trial found everything in readiness.

Anna Siebert was the first witness called by the prosecution.

The bereaved girl avoided Hap Kingman's gaze as she took the stand, was sworn in, and told her brief, tragic story in a voice that shook at times with emotion.

"He seemed all agitated when I saw him—asked me where my father was," the girl testified. "No, he wasn't drunk. Just . . . just angry. His eyes were—like a lion's."

"Did you hear your father quarreling with Kingman?"

"I heard indistinct voices. I was inside the house. Just as I was going out on the porch, I heard the shot."

The prosecuting attorney rubbed his spade beard thoughtfully.

"Did you . . . er . . . actually *see* Kingman shoot your father?"

Anna Siebert paused, brow knitted in thought. The tense courtroom held its breath, intent on her words which might possibly be the keynote of the entire trial.

"No. No—in honesty I cannot say I did. But I . . . I came around the corner just as my father toppled dead from his wheelchair. An instant after the shot was fired."

"Was smoke coming from the defendant's pistol?" Judge Peddicord asked sharply.

Anna Siebert looked puzzled.

"I really can't say. I don't remember. There was a wind sweeping across the porch—if there was much smoke, I would have remembered. It must have blown away. I don't know."

Hap Kingman's heart raced with new hope. He glanced at Russ Melrose, who nodded imperceptibly. The girl's testimony bore out what the cowboy already knew was true. The shot that had killed her father came from somewhere removed from the ranchhouse porch.

"What did you do when you saw your father was killed?"

"I happened to be carrying a quirt. I struck Kingman over the head with it. Then I screamed for the men to come and help me. But it was too late. Daddy was . . . dead."

No further testimony was brought out during Melrose's brief cross-examination.

One by one, several Triangle S punchers testified to finding their veteran employer dead. Then Doc Hanson, the county coroner, gave his technical report regarding the cause of Siebert's death—a bullet in the heart. Death had been instantaneous.

After a noon recess, Hap Kingman himself was placed on the stand. His plea—"Not guilty"—caused a near riot in the courtroom, bursts of cheering from his friends being counteracted by angry yells from Siebert's Triangle S cowhands.

When Judge Peddicord had calmed the courtroom on threat of clearing out the public during the duration of the trial, the prosecuting attorney fired a point-blank question at the cowboy on the stand:

"Did you have any reason to have killed George Siebert?"

For a long moment, Hap Kingman was silent. His eyes shot from Anna Siebert, at the prosecution table, to his lawyer, Russ Melrose. Then, gripping the arms of the witness chair, the cowboy said in a voice like dripping ice:

"Yes. I went out to the ranch to kill Siebert. But I *didn't* kill him."

The prosecuting attorney looked startled. Judge Peddicord sat up with a jerk. An air of tension filled the courtroom.

"Why did you want to kill Siebert? Had he ever wronged you in any way?"

Smoldering hate made pools of light behind Hap Kingman's slitted lids.

"Siebert killed my father. Murdered him. Eighteen years ago, when I was a little tike. Siebert shot my mother in cold blood. I remember it. And I swore to kill Siebert some day."

Again the judge had to pound his gavel for silence. Even the prosecuting attorney seemed overwhelmed by the drama which gripped the courtroom.

"You see," continued Hap Kingman, "my father was Dev Hewett. I'm not a Kingman. The old sheriff and Mrs. Kingman raised me and Everett. It wasn't until . . . until the day of the murder . . . that I found out who killed my parents eighteen years ago. When I found out it was Siebert . . . I . . . I went out to kill him."

"You understand you are on trial for your life, Mr. Kingman!" cried the shocked judge. "Can you prove what you are saying?"

Hap Kingman pointed a shaking finger at Russ Melrose.

"Ask my lawyer. He knew my dad. Ask him if Siebert didn't murder Dev Hewett! Ask him if Dev Hewett didn't will me his six-gun to kill Siebert with!"

The panting cowboy was dismissed from the stand, and the Mexitex courtroom had the unprecedented excitement of seeing a defense lawyer sworn in as a witness for the prosecution. The county attorney rubbed his palms together in glee at the prospect of grilling the buzzard-necked attorney.

In halting words, seemingly torn from his throat against his will, Russ Melrose gave an eloquent portrayal of history—how the dying outlaw, Dev Hewett, had put his son in Melrose's keeping. How that son had grown up, adopted by Sheriff

Les Kingman, to be Hap Kingman, now on trial for his life.

"I tried to dissuade the defendant from going out to Siebert's until he'd thought things over," finished Melrose lamely. "But he'd been brooding all his life, wanting revenge against Dev Hewett's killer. I figure he was crazy when he shot George. Hap really isn't a murderer at heart. He's a good boy, an upstanding citizen."

Above the hubbub which grew to pandemonium in the courtroom, the voice of Dr. Harry Hanson was lifted.

"May I question the witness?" yelled the cow-town medico, when he was finally recognized by the court.

Russ Melrose paled, as he saw the agitation in Hanson's face. Then he relaxed, as he heard Peddicord sustain the prosecution's objection that the medico could be quizzed in due turn.

The court took an adjournment, and Hap Kingman was taken back to jail by Sheriff Reynolds.

Russ Melrose left the courthouse and hurried to his living quarters over the Purple Hawk Saloon. There he downed three fingers of whiskey, to quiet his shaking nerves.

He had hardly finished doing so when a rap sounded at his door and Doc Hanson stepped in.

"There's somethin' damned fishy in the air, Russ!" snapped the coroner, drawing up a chair and staring at the unnerved lawyer. "Why did you get up in court and state on oath that Hap Kingman was the son o' Dev Hewett?"

The lawyer smirked.

"I only told the facts," he said. "Dev Hewett put Hap in my keeping, before he died. That was eighteen years ago. I saw to it that Hap got a good home with Sheriff Kingman."

Doc Hanson snorted with contempt.

"Well, you're loco, Russ. I happen to know that Dev Hewett's son was named Everett. I reckon I'm the only person, outside of yourself, who knows that Everett Kingman, Hap's twin brother, is really Everito Hewett, the *mestizo* son of that outlaw that Siebert shot while Hewett was rustlin' beef."

Melrose gulped hard, thankful for the fiery whiskey that was steadying his nerves. He continued staring at the rawboned little doctor.

"Futhermore," said Hanson, "I was the doctor who was with Hap's mother when she died, in my office. At that very moment, Dev Hewett's corpse was on a slab in my back room."

The doctor stood up, pointed an accusing hand at Melrose.

"You're trying to railroad your own client into a hang noose, Melrose. I don't know what your crooked game is, but I intend to air what I know at court tomorrow. You baited Hap into thinkin' he was Dev Hewett's son, so's he'd kill George

Siebert. And I got a hunch you had good reason for wantin' George murdered."

Melrose thrust a hand into his coat pocket, closed fingers about the haft of a knife he carried there. Unseen inside the pocket, the lawyer's fingers opened the knife.

"By the time I'm through testifyin' to what I know to be true," challenged Doc Hanson, his hand on Melrose's doorknob, "that murder charge will be blown wide open. An' I wouldn't be surprised, Melrose, if your career as a crooked shyster blows up with it!"

Hanson turned to leave, then jerked under the shock of the hard-flung knife which zipped across the room to embed itself to the hilt between his shoulder blades.

Before the coroner had time to topple floorward, Melrose had leaped to his side to cushion his fall.

Yanking the knife from Hanson's back, the lawyer stabbed the medico again and again until he was sure that life was extinct in the only witness who knew the secret of Hap Kingman's strangely tangled past—

8

SURPRISE BY NIGHT

ONLY a cruising Texas moon and a low-winging night owl witnessed the dire actions of Russ Melrose long after midnight had come and gone.

The west wall of the Purple Hawk Saloon was blotted in shadow when the lawyer cautiously opened the window of his room and proceeded to lower a bulky object wrapped in a canvas tarp to the ground below, by means of a reata.

Sliding down the rope which he had tied to a bedpost, Melrose shouldered the canvas-shrouded corpse of Harry Hanson and made his way like a black phantom down the shadow-clogged alleyway which led toward the river.

There were no eyes to see him as he carried his grisly burden along the high adobe wall of a livery barn and thence out of sight inside the board fence of the long-abandoned Texas Queen Copper Co.'s smelter.

Memories almost two decades old swarmed in Melrose's brain as he staggered on with the gruesome load, skirting the slag dump of the defunct mining outfit. He was retracing the footsteps he had made eighteen years before, that grim night of death when he had invaded the Allen prairie schooner.

The futility of that murderous journey had tormented Russ Melrose's dreams in those years. All the reward he had, for filling two graves in boothill, was a worthless gold-mine chart—a map which was still kept in his office safe.

Reaching the dwarf willows along the Rio Grande's bank, Melrose opened the shroud and filled the extra space around the coroner's stiffened corpse with chunks of copper slag and smooth rocks.

Then he lashed the mummy-shaped bundle with rope, and carried it out on a low wooden wharf built out from the copper mining company's land.

Bullfrogs stopped croaking momentarily, startled by the splash of the dead doctor's weighted body plunging into the deepest pool along the north bank of the Rio.

Relief ballooned Melrose's cheeks, as he saw the corpse vanish into the murky depths, saw the ripples gradually smooth out again.

Not until Judgment Day would Harry Hanson's body be seen or heard of again. The catfish might nibble through rotting canvas, but it was doubtful. Coroner Hanson's disappearance would tickle the imagination of the town for a while, but a year from now it would be forgotten, a curious incident in the lurid annals of Yaqui County.

"A year from now!" Russ Melrose whispered the words like an oath, as he made his way back through the moon's witch-glow, heading for his hotel.

A year from now, he would be in control of Siebert's cattle kingdom. He, Russ Melrose, would quit the law business forever, to ramrod the destinies of Yaqui County. And maybe, someday, be the Governor of the Lone Star State.

His sleep that night was untroubled by the fact that a man had died by his hand in his very bedroom. The murder of Harry Hanson had put the last obstacle out of his way, toward the realization of his dreams of a cattle empire.

When Judge Peddicord called the court into session again at nine o'clock, Russ Melrose was on hand alongside of the defendant, Hap Kingman.

If the lawyer's face had blue pockets under the eyes and he seemed a trifle the worse for loss of sleep, no one appeared to notice. After all, Melrose was about to lose a case, a damaging blow to his prestige. Melrose was famous for arguing guilty criminals out of a death cell—for a price.

"The way things went yesterday—you acting like a blabber-mouthed idiot and forcing me to testify against you—I don't think we can hope for a verdict of not guilty," Melrose whispered to Kingman. "We'll have to throw ourselves on the mercy of the court, and hope for a life term."

The cowboy shrugged. He twisted in his chair, to search the sea of spectators' faces for a trace of Everett Kingman, the boy he had grown up with.

He had seen no trace of Everett, had not seen him since they had listened to Mrs. Kingman's will being read in Melrose's office.

A pang of disappointment came to Hap Kingman. He and his blond-haired brother had never gotten along particularly well, but it grieved him to know that the only kin he had—even kin by adoption—was not on hand for the concluding day of his trial.

"I'm not afraid to die," grunted Hap Kingman. "All that galls me is dyin' without findin' out who took a pot shot at George Siebert. That's all."

The prosecuting attorney summed up his case against Hap Kingman, showing the notch-butted six-gun to the jury—the gun which had been Dev Hewett's legacy to his orphan child. The prosecutor, knowing he had the case in the bag, made no capital of the mysterious notches on the backstrap of the six-gun.

He dwelt heavily on the fact that a fired shell was in Kingman's gun; that while Anna Siebert had not actually witnessed the murder of her father, circumstances pointed inexorably to the defendant's guilt.

That, and Hap Kingman's frank avowal that

he had ridden out to the Triangle S with the intention of killing George Siebert, plus the fact that Hap was the half-breed son of a notorious killer of a generation before, were the keynotes of the prosecutor's case.

Russ Melrose, summing up the defense for his client, made an extremely poor showing. He pointed out that the county coroner, Doc Hanson, had been on the point of asking him some questions the day before.

What was Hanson trying to bring into the record? Did the coroner know something that might shed some light on the case? If so, where was Hanson now?

A search of the courtroom failed to reveal the coroner. An illiterate Mexican in the audience played into Melrose's hand by vouchsafing the suggestion that the doctor must be on the Mexican side of the river, delivering a baby for Señora Rosita Inez y Castabello, twenty miles up the Rio.

At any rate, Doc Hanson was absent from Mexitex. If he had had any important knowledge of the case on trial, the prosecutor sneeringly pointed out to the judge, then he would have at least taken the trouble to be on hand.

Russ Melrose, his shoulders slumping in well-feigned resignation, let the case for the defense rest.

With judicial brevity, Judge Peddicord of Del

Rio summed up the case, counselling the jury not to let personal prejudices or friendship for either George Siebert or the defendant have any sway on their verdict.

When the twelve jurymen filed out, Hap Kingman was conscious, for the first time, that Anna Siebert was watching him closely. Tenderness and pity seemed to have replaced the hate and grief in her eyes, as she returned the cowboy's glance.

The room froze with excitement when the door of the jury chamber opened, scarcely five minutes after they had gone into conference. Their decision was plainly written on their faces.

As if from a great distance, Hap Kingman heard the spokesman of the jury croak out the inevitable verdict:

"We find the defendant, Hap Kingman, guilty o' murder in the first degree, as charged by the State o' Texas—"

The cowboy was once more conscious of Anna Siebert's following eyes as the sheriff led him, handcuffed, to a position in front of Judge Peddicord's bench.

But there was no trace of concern or alarm in Hap Kingman's bearing, as he locked glances with the cow-town judge and heard Peddicord address him:

"You have heard the verdict of a jury of your peers, Mr. Kingman. Does the defendant have anything to say in his own behalf before sentence is passed?"

Kingman straightened his shoulders, turned, and with his eyes burning into Anna Siebert's, he said mechanically:

"I've done a lot of thinkin' since I woke up in the calaboose. I can see where I shouldn't have harbored hate all my life against the man who killed my parents in cold blood. It was a force stronger than my own good character, I reckon."

He saw Anna Siebert avert her gaze, press her hands to her face.

"I reckon George Siebert paid plenty for what he did. I understand he didn't know a moment's rest, from his leg wound, since the day he shot Dev Hewett. And I'm sorry for the grief that an innocent girl is sufferin' now."

Turning back to the judge, Hap Kingman raised his voice and said defiantly:

"I'm still sayin' it wasn't my bullet that killed George Siebert, yore honor. I admit I can't prove that, never could. All I'm hopin' is that, after I'm gone, maybe the real killer will be brought to justice. And I'm hopin' someday Anna Siebert can say, 'I'm sorry I called Hap Kingman a murderer.' "

The judge cleared his throat noisily, and slammed his bone-handled gavel on the bench.

"By virtue of the authority vested in me by the people of the Commonwealth of Texas, I hereby sentence you to be hanged by the neck until dead, date of said execution to be tomorrow at the hour of high noon. May the Almighty God have mercy on your soul."

The low sound of Anna Siebert's muffled sob was the only noise that disturbed the ghastly quiet of the Yaqui County bar of justice.

9

SURPRISE BY NIGHT

SLEEP refused to come to Hap Kingman, as he lay on the blanketless cot of his jail cell.

Throughout the long hours leading up to midnight he had heard the sound of revelry in the Mexitex saloons, as carousing Triangle S punchers celebrated the death sentence which had been imposed.

Disinterested spectators at the trial had greeted the verdict with applause, likewise. The slaying of a crippled man in a wheelchair did not set well with Westerners.

The town's squalid hotels and shabby rooming houses were jammed to capacity with visitors waiting overnight to be on hand for the morrow's hanging.

Visitors were denied the condemned man, although Hap knew that Anna Siebert had tried to get to him late that afternoon.

In the excitement following the verdict, no tongue voiced the question about what had become of the county coroner, old Sawbones Hanson. It was unlikely that anyone outside of

Melrose, the defense lawyer, even noticed the old medico's absence.

The jail was shared by some drunken cowboys who had tanked up beyond their rated alcoholic capacity at the Purple Hawk and had been jailed by Sheriff Bob Reynolds, and by a Mexican, who was being held by the border patrol for unlawful entry into the United States. The latter tried to soothe Kingman's fast-fleeting hours of life with his guitar and uncertain baritone.

The din lulled after midnight. The sky was overcast and there was a hint of rain in the atmosphere, as the cow town turned in with hopes that Kingman's day of execution would not be marred by an unseasonal shower.

Two hours before daylight was due, four ghostly figures materialized from the direction of the Rio Grande and made their stealthy way to the jailhouse.

They wore the serapes and cone-peaked sombreros of Mexicans, and their *zapato*-clad feet made no sound as they skirted the jailhouse to make sure no guards were posted at the rear door.

Entering the sheriff's office, the four found grim-faced Bob Reynolds propped up against the cell-block door with a sawed-off shotgun across his knees.

"*Que estan?*" demanded the sheriff, blinking in the glow of his low-wicked desk lamp as the four Mexicans stood facing him, their stolid faces blank of expression. "If you greasers have come to visit that guitar-playin' alien, you can rattle your hocks. No visitin' allowed as long as Señor Kingman is bein' held here. Go on—*vente*! Vamoose!"

The Mexican quartet turned to go, and Bob Reynolds settled his chin on his chest to resume his doze.

Things happened fast, then.

One of the Mexicans hurled out his poncho, draping it over the sheriff's head and shoulders, while a second pounced for the gun on Reynold's lap.

A third whipped a six-gun from under his serape and the heavy butt smashed against the sheriff's skull, the blow padded by the smothering poncho which the leader had wrapped about the lawman's neck.

It was all over in an instant.

Stretching out the unconscious sheriff, one of the Mexicans frisked Reynolds to produce a ring of jail keys.

A moment's sorting through the keys and the Mexican unlocked the cell-block door and padded inside, scratching a match and peering into each cell in turn.

The drunken cowboys were sleeping off their jag. The guitar-playing alien, faced with a prison term if he was deported by the border patrol, grinned smugly as he recognized fellow country-men.

But the Mexican leader struck a new match and proceeded around the cells until he came to one where a chap-clad cowboy was smoking a cigarette in the solitude of his steel-barred cage.

"Señor Kingman?"

"Yeah."

"*Bueno.*"

Hap Kingman's jaw dropped with an oath of surprise as he saw the Mexican unlock his cell door and motion for him to come.

Unprotesting, his heart leaping with a new lease on life, the condemned buckaroo hurried out after the Mexican, his eyes widening with surprise as he saw the knocked-out sheriff.

"What in hell—"

The Mexicans motioned for him to be silent. One of them blew out Reynolds' lamp, while the others padded silently out into the night.

Before the lamp went out, Hap Kingman caught sight of Dev Hewett's cedar-butted Colt Peacemaker lying on the sheriff's desk—the .45-calibered legacy that had been the exhibit in his murder trial.

Kingman caught up the six-gun and thrust it inside the waistband of his bullhide chaps, before accompanying his rescuer outside.

The Mexicans moved off toward the river, padding along the jail wall in Indian file.

Not asking questions, unable to fathom who these swarthy-skinned benefactors could be, Hap Kingman crept along with them.

Skirting wide to avoid the low bridge which formed the official port of entry across the Rio Grande, the spokesman of the Mexican four turned to whisper to Kingman:

"Be very careful, señor. If the *federalistas* know we cross the border, it is *muy malo*."

Kingman nodded. He knew the vigilant eye of the border patrol would be on the alert for border hoppers, at any hour of the twenty-four.

Through the blackness of the Texas night, Kingman followed his mysterious helpers to dense willows at the river's edge, and out across the mud to where a crude raft had been moored to a protruding boulder.

The four crawled aboard the raft, Kingman in their midst.

With stout poles, the Mexicans shoved the raft silently out onto the freshet-swollen current of the muddy Rio.

The river caught the craft, turning it slowly in the flood.

Kingman crouched on his haunches, his pulse racing.

He saw the lights of Mexitex slip from sight as the current bore them downstream, around the curving shale cliffs.

Not until the muddy stream had carried them a

full mile from town did Hap Kingman venture the question that had been hammering at his mind:

"Who are you, anyway? I didn't know I had any Mexican amigos who would risk their hides to—"

The strange hombres grunted for him to be silent, to wait.

On and on the raft drifted. Two miles. Three. Chihuahua's rugged hills glided by to the southwest; at Kingman's left elbow were the low Texas cliffs.

He recognized the pile of rocks which marked the boundary between his own Flying K ranch and the range belonging to George Siebert's vast syndicate.

Then, at a point opposite the Triangle S ranch and fully five miles by crowflight from the border town, the Mexicans began poling the raft out of the sluggish current, toward a cactus-crowned bluff on the Mexican bank.

The sickle-shaped moon broke through the scudding clouds as the raft grated on a sandbar, to reveal heavy, dank brush choking the edge of the Rio Grande.

The Mexicans, grunting for Kingman to follow, splashed ashore through ankle-deep mud and burrowed into the chaparral.

The mouth of a low cavern loomed against the chalky gray cliff, and as Hap Kingman followed wonderingly in the steps of his deliverers, he saw a sombreroed figure bowleg his way out to meet them.

Kingman halted, as he saw the chap-legged figure dismiss the Mexicans with a grunt of approval.

"Howdy, Hap. How does it feel to have a hangman's rope yanked offn your throat?"

Hap's jaw sagged in astonishment. The speaker was his missing foster-brother, Everett Kingman.

10

OWLHOOT ORDERS

THE rescued cowboy rushed forward to thrust out a hand to Everett Kingman. The coal of the latter's cigarette ebbed and glowed in the darkness, and Hap saw the pale glitter of his brother's teeth exposed in a smile.

"What . . . what does this mean, Everett?" whispered the cowboy. "I don't get it. How'd you find this cave? Who are those Mexicans?"

Everett Kingman flicked his quirly butt into the mud, ground it out under heel. Then he took Hap's arm.

"Come inside—can't risk the patrol riders spottin' us from the American bank," his brother stated. "There's a lot you don't know, Hap. You may as well know now."

Puzzled by Everett's enigmatical words, Hap Kingman allowed himself to be led into the black maw of the cavern at cliff's base. The inky throat of the tunnel turned at right angles after a few yards, opening into a limestone chamber as big as a house.

Light was provided by a number of lanterns.

Hap Kingman was startled to see that the cave was outfitted for human occupancy, with bedrolls on mattresses of dried brush, and mangers built of planks for a half dozen horses at the far end of the subterranean room.

"I'll be damned!" The wondering cowboy chuckled, as Everett led him up to a crude pine table littered with playing cards and whiskey bottles. "Looks like a reg'lar robbers' roost, or somethin'."

Everett grunted, seating himself on a powder box in lieu of a chair and waving his brother onto another box.

"This is where you'll hole up until this jail break blows over, kid," grunted Everett, lighting up a tapering black-paper Mexican cigarette.

Hap Kingman grinned with relief. Not until now could he bring himself to believe the fantastic fact that he was not going to trip a gallows trap at high noon tomorrow.

"How'd you work it, anyhow?" he asked. "I wondered why you weren't at the trial. And I reckon I can never repay you for savin' my life, Everett."

Low guffaws from the Mexicans who squatted about a tiny fire nearby made Kingman's eyes swing to study the peculiar grin on his brother's face. It was not a pleasant grin.

"You'll pay me back, all right, kid," slurred

Everett Kingman. "*Es seguro*! I was comin' to that."

"What do you mean?" Kingman's voice was low, puzzled.

"Did you think for a minute," sneered Everett Kingman, "that I risked my men's lives to snatch you out o' that *juzgado* just because we was raised together?"

Hap leaned forward, a scowl gathering between his brows.

"Put your cards on the table, Everett!" he demanded. "What are you drivin' at? Why do you call these hombres your men?"

Everett Kingman leaned over to open a small pair of saddlebags on the table. He drew forth several small tin cans, and brown glass bottles which glittered in the lantern light.

"These cans are full o' opium, to sell to the chinks who work in the Arizona mines," was Everett's astonishing disclosure. "These bottles contain morphine, cocaine."

Hap stared aghast at the contraband, as comprehension dawned slowly and reluctantly within him.

"You mean—this is a smugglin' gang's headquarters? You mean to tell me, Everett, that you're a *contrabandisto*?"

Everett exposed yellow-stained teeth in a leer.

"How else would I get the dinero to gamble with, to buy liquor an' treat the señoritas with?

Not from what I earned from our damned Flyin' K spread." He inhaled deeply. "Hap, you might as well know that I'm the *segundo*—the right-hand man of the smugglin' chief, Señor Giboso. An' I have been, ever since I was seventeen."

Señor Giboso! The name made Hap Kingman sway as if struck by a hammer. Señor Giboso was the name of an elusive smuggler who had terrorized the Rio Grande country for ten years; a masked smuggler who had slipped through the fingers of the Mexican rurales and the American border officers on countless occasions, usually leaving dead men behind him. *Sheriff Kingman had been one of them.*

It was almost too much to comprehend. And yet these sinister-visaged Mexicans, this well-hidden rendezvous, all bore out Everett's frank confession.

"Why are you tellin' me this, Everett?"

His brother leaned forward, twin ropes of smoke dribbling from his nostrils.

"Why not? You're goin' to join us, Hap. Don't forget you're an escaped murderer in the eyes of the law. There'll be a reward posted on your head, dead or alive. You ain't in any position to balk. You'll help us smuggle contraband, or—"

Everett left his sentence unfinished, but its implication of swift doom was clear enough.

Hap Kingman's face drained of color as he leaped to his feet, jaw outthrust, hand dropping to the cedar handle of Dev Hewett's deadly six-gun.

Everett did not flicker an eyelash or twitch a muscle, but behind him the four Mexicans leaped to their feet, knives flashing in the lantern shine, naked gun barrels glittering.

"What if I refuse to become a smuggler, Everett?"

Everett shrugged.

"You wouldn't get out o' this cave alive, for one thing. Besides, kid—don't you owe us somethin' for gettin' you out o' jail tonight?"

Hap Kingman slowly relaxed his taut muscles. He seemed ringed about by leveled guns, glittering eyes. He was helpless, enmeshed in a criminal web from which there could be no escape.

"All right," he husked out finally. "I'll work for you and Señor Giboso—on one job. Then I'm quittin', and you can shoot me or be damned. Maybe I am an outlaw. Maybe they will post a bounty for my capture. But I'm no smuggler, Everett, and never will be."

Everett Kingman motioned for his swart-skinned henchmen to sheath their weapons.

"I knew you'd see it my way, kid," he purred menacingly. "You'll lay low for three or four days, an' then I'm sendin' you to Señor Giboso for further orders, savvy? We need a man who can use his guns—who'll have to shoot to save his own hide. That's why I saw to it that you didn't swing for Siebert's murder."

In the ghastly quiet of the dank cavern, Everett's pronouncement was more sinister than Judge Peddicord's death sentence had been—and infinitely more positive.

Anna Siebert returned to her home on the Triangle S immediately after the sheriff had refused her a chance of talking with the condemned prisoner, Hap Kingman.

She spent a troubled night, tortured by nightmares of seeing the clean-cut young puncher dangling at rope's end for the slaying of her father.

Next morning, after a breakfast which threatened to nauseate her, the girl found herself drawn by some strangely impelling force to the north porch of the ranchhouse, to the place where George Siebert had gone to his doom.

Shuddering, Anna Siebert averted her eyes from the spot where her father had been smoking peacefully in his wheelchair. She gripped a stucco-plastered porch pillar for support, her eyes suddenly blinded with tears.

Then it was that the syndicate owner's daughter caught sight of something on the smooth surface of the porch post which brought her nerves tinglingly alive.

One corner of the post had been chipped off,

and the faint trace of a furrow had been grooved along the smooth plaster, at a slight angle off horizontal.

It was a recently made bullet track. Instinct told Anna Siebert that it could be nothing else.

"I wonder . . . it can't be—"

The girl's heart seemed to freeze within her as she unconsciously followed the angle of the tiny furrow downward, saw that it lined up with the exact spot where George Siebert had been sitting at the time of his death.

With a low cry, Anna Siebert turned about to face outdoors, and knelt for a moment to squint along the bullet furrow in the porch post as she might peer down the sights on a gun barrel.

The bullet's angle led her eye to a clump of buckthorn brush on the skyline of Manzanita Hill, the hog-back ridge which overlooked the ranchhouse.

Hardly conscious of what she was doing, the girl ran down the porch steps and off across the lawn, keeping her eyes fixed on the clump of buckthorn chaparral.

Pushing open the yard gate, she began scrambling up the steep rocky slope of Manzanita Hill, with a goat-like agility which she had mastered during her girlhood. She had climbed this hill a thousand times, at play.

Now her face was set in grim lines as she climbed doggedly, clinging to sagebrush clumps and manzanita scrub for support, her boots slogging on the flinty soil, pounding on sun-dried adobe.

Five minutes later she had gained the ridge crest.

Her heart was beating furiously as she pushed her way through the buckthorn brush.

Then she halted, her eyes riveted to a shimmering piece of metal which the sun's rays picked up, a piece of furbished brass which shed dazzling spears of reflected light.

Leaping forward, Anna Siebert snatched up the metal object. It was a center-fire .30-30-calibered cartridge case, empty of powder or bullet.

Not until then did Anna Siebert notice something else.

The Texas sun had dried the adobe mud which the previous week's rains had formed on the crest of Manzanita Hill. And that sloppy ooze, hardening, had held fast the molded imprint of a man's hob-nailed boots, the indentations in the mud where the knees of a kneeling man had pressed.

She followed the tracks, down the east slope of the ridge, reading sign like an Indian scout as she came to the marks of a horse's hoofs. The horse tracks led off in the direction of Mexitex town.

Anna Siebert wasted no time then. She raced back to the ranchhouse, and gave swift orders for a *mozo* to saddle a fast pony for her.

Ten minutes later found the girl spurring at full

gallop along the tree-bordered lane, heading for Mexitex town in the distance.

The hour was yet early, so that few men moved on the main street as she flung herself from saddle in front of Doc Hanson's office and undertaking parlors.

Bursting through the door, Anna Siebert recognized the deputy coroner, Dan Kendelhardt.

"Where's Dr. Hanson, Dan?" she asked breathlessly. "I've got to see him—at once!"

Kendelhardt scratched his head.

"That's what I been wonderin', Miss Siebert. Doc ain't been in for two nights. It's got me worried. He ain't out on a call, because his kitbag is in the closet there. It's not like Doc to vamoose without leavin' word with me."

Anna Siebert gripped the young undertaker's wrist.

"Listen, Dan," she said hoarsely. "You . . . you'd have the authority . . . to perform an autopsy on my dad's body, wouldn't you?"

"I reckon so, Miss Siebert. But the . . . that is, the cause of death is known. Gunshot wound. Doc Hanson—"

Brushing tears from her eyes, Anna forced herself to go on:

"I want you to probe out the bullet that killed daddy, and do it quick. A . . . a man's life may depend on it. I can't wait for Doc Hanson to show up and do the job."

Kendelhardt started to protest, and then turned and vanished inside the morgue room.

For the better part of a half-hour, Anna Siebert paced the doctor's office in an agony of tortured emotions. Her face was white and spent when Kendelhardt finally re-entered the room, bearing a white towel draped across one hand.

Cradled on the towel was a twisted blob of metal, jacketed in a case of cuprous steel.

" 'Pears to be a .30-30 slug, Miss Siebert. Fired from a rifle. Six-guns don't shoot steel-jacketed bullets."

Controlling herself with difficulty, Anna Siebert pressed into the deputy coroner's hand the bright cartridge case she had found on the crest of Manzanita Hill, above her father's home.

"Run over to the jail and give this to Sheriff Reynolds, Dan!" she gasped hysterically. "Tell him what you found. Tell him to cancel Hap Kingman's hanging, do you understand? We've got to have a new trial—"

Understanding seized Kendelhardt, made him mouth a low oath and then reach for his hat on a nearby peg. A moment later he was gone, sprinting at top speed toward the jail building.

A violent reaction seized Anna Siebert then, and she was just recovering from her hysterical weeping when Kendelhardt came back to the doctor's office, ten minutes later.

"All hell—beggin' your pardon, Miss Siebert—

busted loose last night!" panted the excited deputy coroner. "Somebody knocked out the sheriff, and Hap Kingman escaped. Busted jail! Bob Reynolds an' a posse are out scourin' the country for him, now!"

Anna Siebert pressed a trembling hand to her breast, and closed her eyes as she leaned against the coroner for support.

"Thank God! Thank God," she whispered brokenly. "We almost . . . sent an innocent man . . . to the gallows, Dan."

11

SEÑOR GIBOSO

AFTER three days of hiding out in the Rio Grande cavern headquarters of his brother, Hap Kingman left under cover of a cloud-blanketed night for an obscure inland town named Maduro, from the fig trees which flanked its plaza.

With his speaking knowledge of Spanish, the gringo cowboy had no difficulty in locating the *posada* where Everett had told him Señor Giboso would be found.

On presentation of a password, the innkeeper bade Hap Kingman wait a short period in the lobby, before taking him up a flight of steps to a dimly lighted room in the rear of the Mexican hotel.

There, his eyes blinked by a kerosene lamp backed by a nickel-plated reflector, Hap Kingman faced for the first time the sinister border character who had been dubbed "Giboso" because his spine was misshapen and humped—Giboso being Mexican jargon for "the hump-backed one."

Squinting at the dazzling light, Kingman saw

the malformed smuggler boss seated behind a table, his face hidden by the shadow of a steeple-peaked sombrero, features masked with a flung-over hem of his gaudy serape.

Without speaking, the cowboy tendered a brief letter of introduction from Everett, which Señor Giboso accepted with a gloved hand and read swiftly in the lamplight.

"Ah, *si*," whispered Señor Giboso, in a voice which sounded to Kingman like a reptile's hiss. "You will make a good *contrabandista*, Señor Kingman. Your *hermano*'s letter tells me you are a desperado wanted by gringo sheriffs, for murder."

Kingman flushed angrily.

"I'm goin' to deliver one shipment of dope for you in Mexitex's native quarter. I promised my brother I'd do that much, because he saved my life," snarled the cowboy. "Then I'm on my own. I wasn't cut out for this owlhoot business— especially not for trafficking in narcotics."

Señor Giboso's intake of breath sounded like hissing steam in the ill-smelling room, but without comment the deformed smuggler passed over a pair of saddlebags which were packed with what Hap knew to be narcotic contraband.

"You will deliver this to the *casa* of Juan Fernandez, on the Avenida de las Palmas, in Mexitex," ordered Señor Giboso, still speaking in his oily whisper. "Everett will give you further orders, and payment for this work. I have no doubt, Señor, that you will reconsider. Once a smuggler for Señor Giboso, always a smuggler, my gringo friend—if you want to keep on living long."

Kingman shouldered the saddlebags, clamped on his sombrero, and strode out of the room. He was glad to be rid of the smuggler chief's presence; the very atmosphere was shot with evil, giving Kingman the impression of wallowing in a sewer, consorting with some foul breed of rat.

His face was covered now with a week's scrub of beard, but he had little fear of seeing anyone in Maduro town who had attended his trial in Mexitex the week before.

Grimly remounting the cayuse which Everett had loaned him, Hap Kingman spurred out of the town and headed northward along a winding trail which snaked through the cactus-dotted Chihuahua badlands.

He passed dingy-looking peons driving ox carts or mounted on burros, during the day; but they gave the gringo no more than a passing glance. Still Kingman knew that the only gringos who ever frequented Maduro town were Americans wanted by the law north of the border.

As he rode, many thoughts tangled in Kingman's mind. His future plans were vague, indefinable.

A week ago he had been conducting the

business of his foster parents' Flying K ranch, with little on his mind save the ever-present, subconscious thirst for revenge which had been in the back of his head ever since that terrible night during the third year of his life when he had seen a red-masked killer shoot his father and mother.

Strangely enough, the death of George Siebert gave Kingman little satisfaction. He realized, now, that the fulfillment of revenge brought little solace to a human heart. Siebert's death would not restore his slain parents to him.

"I'm glad I didn't fire the bullet that killed him," he found himself admitting out loud. "At any rate, I'm not a murderer, even if the State of Texas thinks I am. My conscience is free enough."

And then another thought struck the unhappy cowboy. If his father was named Dev Hewett, then his name was Hewett likewise. But he could not remember his father. His father's place had been taken by the kindly, generous old Texas sheriff named Les Kingman.

Out of respect for that foster-father's loving care and fatherly companionship during his adolescent years, Hap knew the least he could do to thank Sheriff Kingman for all he had done was to retain Kingman's name.

He had brought dishonor and disgrace to that proud Texas name, it was true; but the clearing of that name gave him something to live for now. And—although the cowboy might not have realized it—he would not know a peaceful moment until Anna Siebert knew the truth about her father's death; knew that he was no common killer, taking human life without compunction.

Thus ran the trend of Hap Kingman's thought, as he saw the darkness of the Mexican night overtaking him five miles south of Mexitex.

He was firmly resolved not to continue working with Señor Giboso's smuggling ring, despite the hunch-backed chieftain's grim threat of personal revenge if he quit their ranks.

He would turn over this night's shipment of contraband to the waiting Mexican accomplice, Juan Fernandez; and then he would be through. And if Everett should ever cross his trail and seek to blackmail him into outlaw servitude for assisting him out of jail, Hap knew that he would return Everett's bullets in kind.

During his youth, Hap had visited the Mexican side of Mexitex frequently enough to know where the Avenida de las Palmas was located, deep in the shabbiest section of the peon town.

He did not know, as he made inquiries from street loafers, that the home of Juan Fernandez had once been the home of the outlaw he believed to be his father, Dev Hewett. He did not know that Hewett's true offspring, Everito, had been born inside the soot-blackened adobe walls of that thatch-roofed *jacal*.

Dismounting in pitch blackness outside Fernandez's shack, Hap Kingman slung the dope-laden *alforja* bags over a weary shoulder, and knocked at the door of the hut.

A blast of garlic and chili-laden air hit him in the face as a buxom-hipped Mexican woman admitted him. In answer to his request for Juan Fernandez she pointed to one of four Mexicans seated at a table devouring tortilla cakes and mescal.

Fernandez was a towering Mexican, his face a horrid caricature speckled with smallpox scars.

Without bothering to tender Señor Giboso's official password which would identify him as a smuggler, Hap Kingman rasped out words which left a sour taste in his mouth:

"Here's some contraband from Señor Giboso."

Fernandez shoved his chair back from the table as the American flung the saddlebags on the floor with a gesture like ridding himself of a load of decayed garbage.

Only when he saw the startled suspicion on the countenances of Fernandez's three Mexican diners did Hap Kingman realize he had unintentionally revealed to them the fact that their host was a contraband smuggler.

But the verbal slip did not concern Kingman particularly. It was Juan's headache, not his. With a shrug, he turned and stalked out of the ill-smelling hovel.

"Contrabando?" rasped one of Fernandez's guests. "*Porque* does this stranger leave contrabando with you, amigo?"

The smuggler's face twitched with dread. Over in the corner his slovenly wife was trembling visibly. No one in Mexitex had dreamed that her *esposo* was a secret henchman of Señor Giboso's. Now this loose-tongued gringo had given away that deadly secret—

"*Quien sabe?*" answered Fernandez. "But I have seen that gringo's face somewhere. I wonder—"

And then a heaven-sent inspiration came to the smuggler's aid, as he faced the accusing eyes of his guests.

Rushing to a table, the Mexican whipped up a leaflet which had been left at his door—a leaflet similar to hundreds which the rurale police had distributed to the native population of Mexitex.

Fernandez unfolded the paper, and the guttering flames of an oil lamp showed it to be a reward poster written in Spanish:

1,000 PESOS REWARD!
For the capture, dead or alive,
of the American outlaw who
broke jail in Mexitex, named

HAP KINGMAN
Convicted of murder.

113

The poster was signed by Sheriff Bob Reynolds.

Juan Fernandez stabbed a hand under his serape and drew forth a long-barreled .45 revolver. The other men rushed at his heels as Fernandez headed for the door with a hoarse whisper:

"That gringo *vaquero* was Hap Kingman—I saw him at the courthouse trial, *es verdad*!"

Outside, Hap Kingman was busy tightening the latigo of his saddle, preparatory to mounting his horse.

He turned as he heard bare feet slogging out of the door behind him, then gasped as he felt Juan Fernandez jab a six-gun barrel into his ribs.

"What's the idea, Fernandez?"

The Mexican's tequila-fouled breath was hot on Kingman's face as the smuggler snarled:

"You are my prisoner, señor. I am taking you across the border to the Americano sheriff, Señor Bob Reynolds. *Maños arriba, señor*—or I will kill you now, pronto!"

Even with the muzzle of a cocked gun reamed in his short ribs, Hap Kingman felt a swift, hot urge to lash out a fist to Juan Fernandez's jaw in the darkness, and take his chances of the Mexican's trigger finger not blasting him into eternity.

Then, staring off beyond the smuggler's shoulder, he saw the burly forms of Fernandez's peon friends trooping out the *jacal* door behind their host, lamplight glinting on knives and gun barrels.

Even if he could overpower Fernandez, he could not hope to get in saddle and make a getaway.

"*Maños arribas*! Get those hands up, señor!"

The gringo cowpuncher took his hands out from under the saddle skirts where he had been knotting his latigo, and slowly raised his arms.

He felt Fernandez empty his holsters of their guns, frisk him deftly for hidden knife or gun.

Then, backing off a step, the Mexican said to his friends in guttural Spanish:

"Bring the contrabando, Julio. We will take it to the *federalistos*, also. There may be a double reward for capturing Señor Kingman, if they know he is a smuggler likewise!"

The Mexican addressed as Julio rushed inside the shack to emerge a moment later with the saddlebags which Hap Kingman had delivered, per Señor Giboso's orders.

Cold despair had turned the cowboy's spine to an ice pole. Moments before, a new life had loomed before him. He had divorced himself of any connection with Señor Giboso or the diabolical outlaw gang with which his brother Everett had been linked.

Getting across the border at some remote spot along the Rio Grande would have been relatively easy. He knew that anywhere in the cow country, from Mexico to Montana, he could earn a living. In some far-off spot where George Siebert had never been heard of, he could begin life anew. After all, there was nothing more to tie him to Mexitex.

He would gladly relinquish his rightful claim to a part of the Flying K ranch. He had no living relatives that he knew of. The only motive he might have had for remaining in Texas would have been to clear his name of the unjust charge of murder which lay upon it.

But that had all been changed now. He was in the grip of an illiterate, drunken peon, whose greedy eyes saw in his visitor a walking fortune—a gringo with a reward on his scalp. And Hap Kingman knew it would take little provocation for Juan Fernandez to pull trigger and deliver his prize as a corpse instead of on the hoof.

"You win, Fernandez," said the cowboy bitterly. "Let's get goin'."

Señor Fernandez waddled out of the foul-smelling shack with a braided rawhide riata. The three Mexicans who had been eating supper with Fernandez made quick work of tying Kingman's wrists tightly behind his back and lashing his arms to his sides with many turns of the rope.

That done, Fernandez ordered his prisoner to walk up the Avenida de las Palmas, in the direction of the low bridge which linked the south half of Mexitex with the American side of the Rio Grande.

Julio led Kingman's lather-flanked horse, and carried the *alforjas* laden with contraband. Fernandez and the other Mexican marched at Kingman's either elbow, guns drawn, making sure that their quarry make no attempt at bolting into a dark side street.

Reaching the adobe-walled headquarters of the Mexican *rurale* police, on the south end of the Rio Grande bridge, they were halted by a uniformed customs official.

A swift interchange of Spanish occurred, but Kingman paid scant attention. He was a man suddenly without hope, without a future—destined to a quick finish at the bottom end of a hangman's rope.

The Mexican officials chattered excitedly and led Kingman and his horse and his peon guards over to the border patrol headquarters on the American side.

A moment later, Hap Kingman found himself staring at Inspector Gordon Chamberlin, a young border patrolman with whom Kingman had gone to school and played baseball in years past.

"Jumpin' juniper, Hap!" cried Chamberlin, as he held a lantern up to stare into the cowboy's bleak face. "How come you were captured on the Mex side of the Rio?"

Juan Fernandez and his reward-thirsty partners

chattered excitedly to Chamberlin, whose face registered disbelief as he turned once more to the trussed-up cowboy.

"Fernandez here said you were one of Señor Giboso's *compadres*," said the border patrolman incredulously. "How come he says that, Hap?"

The cowboy jerked himself out of his torpor and shrugged.

"I'm in a jam, all right, Gordon. What's the chances of gettin' up to the jailhouse where I won't have to rub shoulders with these smelly greasers?"

Chamberlin turned to the Mexicans, who insisted noisily that they be allowed to accompany their prisoner until he was safe in the custody of gringo law.

Thus it was, ten minutes later, that Inspector Chamberlin escorted Hap Kingman into the jail office. There, a deputy sheriff locked the cowboy in the same cell he had occupied during his trial for George Siebert's murder.

Half an hour later the cell-block door opened to admit three important visitors—Chamberlin, representing the United States Customs; Sheriff Bob Reynolds, his temple still bandaged as a result of the jailbreak episode; and Kingman's lawyer, Russ Melrose.

The sheriff was carrying Señor Giboso's saddlebags, which had been unbuckled and their

118

contents examined. The faces of all three were serious as they entered Kingman's cell and stood facing the cowboy.

Hap glanced at Russ Melrose who was running the point of his tongue across his lips with jerky nervous movements. Kingman's capture after his getaway seemed to have put the cow-town lawyer into a fever of excitement, the nature of which Kingman had no way of guessing.

"Well, Hap, you're back again," commented Bob Reynolds. "As it turned out, your Mexican pards were a bit premature in getting you out of the calaboose. Another few hours and you would have gained a new trial with regards to George Siebert's murder."

Kingman jerked erect, stunned at the sheriff's unexpected words. At the same time he saw Russ Melrose fidgeting nervously.

"Juan Fernandez tells us you brought him these saddlebags tonight, Hap," said the lawyer. "You got any way of explaining that?"

Kingman started to speak, but the sheriff cut him off with a curt rebuke to the lawyer:

"You aren't trying the prisoner, Russ. If there will be any questionin' Hap, me or the inspector here will do it. As Hap's legal counsel, you got a right to listen in an' advise Hap not to talk if you want. But don't you do the questionin'."

Melrose subsided, but his heart relaxed with inner relief at the adroit manner in which he

119

had switched the subject from George Siebert's murder charge.

"About these saddlebags," said Chamberlin. "Those Mexies tried to say you brought them from Señor Giboso, the smuggler. Is that correct, Hap?"

Kingman, elbows on knees, rested his chin in his palms and stared moodily at the cell floor.

"I reckon so, Gordon. Leastwise I got those saddlebags from Señor Giboso."

Gasps of astonishment greeted Kingman's cool confession.

"I don't get it, Hap," said the border patrol officer finally. "Why should you even know Señor Giboso, let alone act as a messenger for him?"

Kingman started to speak, then clamped his lips.

If he explained why he had been cast in the role of a smuggler's accomplice, it would necessitate bringing the name of his foster-brother Everett into the open.

Despite the fact that Everett had held him a virtual prisoner in the Rio Grande cave during the days that Sheriff Reynolds had been combing the country for him, Hap could not speak openly. The ties of long association with the man who had been his twin brother, in the eyes of the rangeland, were too strong to be broken thus easily.

"I . . . I can't tell you that, Gordon."

The young border inspector tapped Señor Giboso's saddlebags with a forefinger.

"Did you know what was inside these bags, Hap?"

Kingman paused. "I didn't open 'em," he said, "but I judge they contained contraband. Dope of some kind."

Sheriff Reynolds laughed throatily.

"That's puttin' it mild. There's a young fortune in morphine and opium in those bags, Hap."

There was a moment's silence, broken only by Russ Melrose's laborious breathing.

"How come you delivered this stuff to Juan Fernandez, Hap?" asked Chamberlin finally.

"Because," said Kingman hopelessly, as he felt the grim meshes of the law tightening about him, "because Señor Giboso told me to deliver 'em to Fernandez. Don't ask me why I contacted Señor Giboso, because I . . . I can't answer that."

Russ Melrose cleared his throat noisily.

"You might as well know, Hap," snarled the lawyer, "that I'm washing my hands of you. I'm not your legal adviser from here on out. If there's anything I don't cotton to it's having dealings with a man who traffics in such stuff as dope."

Kingman, his heart tightening in a knot within him at the hopelessness of his situation, said nothing.

"Fernandez claims he never saw you before,

to speak to, and that he isn't an accomplice of Señor Giboso's," said Gordon Chamberlin. "He says you must have delivered that contraband to his house by mistake. And the fact that he turned over the dope to me seems to bear out the truth of what the Mexican says."

"Yeah," added the sheriff. "The reward posted for your capture was as good on your dead carcass as on the hoof, Hap. If Fernandez was a dope smuggler, he could have kept the dope and shot you, and we'd never've been any the wiser."

Kingman smiled bitterly. He believed he knew the reason why Juan Fernandez was acting as he was. Fernandez had no intention of being branded as one of Señor Giboso's men, in the presence of the Mexicans who had been guests at his home when Kingman had delivered Señor Giboso's dope shipment to him.

"Hap," said Sheriff Reynolds, "you're outside o' my jurisdiction now. I don't mind sayin' it's a surprise to me that you have been revealed as a smuggler, of all things. But I got to hold you now, for the U. S. Customs. And they treat smugglers rough when they got the goods on 'em."

Kingman made no reply as the three men left the jail room. Hap thought that he might be carrying a brother's loyalty too far, in protecting Everett. But he would hang for his original crime, the murder of George Siebert, for which he had been found guilty. There was no use going to his grave with the knowledge that he had mired his own brother in trouble also.

If Everett chose to lead a smuggler's career, retribution might catch up with him sooner or later, anyway.

12

HANGING BEE

LAWYER Russ Melrose left the jail hurriedly, his brain whirling with apprehension.

The news of Hap Kingman's jail break had been enough to rob the lawyer of sleep during the nights that had followed. He believed he knew the cowboy well enough to know that Hap, even though free of the gallows, would make an effort to find out who had really killed George Siebert, and why.

And if that information came to light—

"I got to make sure that Hap's out of the way," decided the lawyer as he made his way toward his living quarters in the upper floor of the Purple Hawk Saloon. "If he finds out that Anna Siebert cleared him of murder guilt by finding a .30-30 bullet in her father's brisket, instead of a six-gun slug—"

Instead of going upstairs to his rooms, the lawyer shouldered his way into the tobacco-clouded barroom of the Purple Hawk. The gambling tables were being patronized by most of Mexitex's rougher characters, border riffraff.

Coarse-visaged men bellied the long pine counter of the Purple Hawk's bar—men straddling the law in many cases, and among them several hombres who would now be breaking rocks in a penitentiary, or filling unmarked graves on boothill, had it not been for Melrose's ability to defend guilty men in court.

Melrose made his way to the bar and took a position alongside a cinnamon-whiskered lobo known as Fanner Sobolo, his nickname arising from his skill at fanning the guns which he carried in thonged-down half-breed holsters at either hip.

"Howdy, Melrose!" gruffed Sobolo, his tongue thick with liquor. "What's new?"

Melrose ordered a drink of rot-gut. Toying with the glass of amber liquor, the lawyer remarked casually:

"Well, Hap Kingman's been captured."

His voice carried along the bar, and instantly a hush descended over the drinkers. Men began crowding close, as the startling word was carried from mouth to mouth along the bar.

"You don't say!" gruffed Fanner Sobolo. "Well, no use me keepin' my eyes peeled for that busky, I reckon. I was hopin' I could get my gunsights on Kingman. I could use the dinero posted on his noggin."

Melrose turned his back to the bar and hooked a heel over the brass rail.

"Yeah, Hap Kingman was captured over on the other side of the Rio," the lawyer went on, his eyes flashing over the faces of his listeners. "He was smuggling dope for Señor Giboso, no less. Got caught carrying contraband!"

Within the minute, gamblers had left their tables and were crowding about the bar, the news on every tongue. The jail break of Hap Kingman had been the most exciting morsel of news in Mexitex for many months.

"I won't be defending Kingman this time," the lawyer went on. "He told me he didn't murder George Siebert, and I took him at his word. But he don't deny being a smuggler—and that's one breed of snake I won't go to court for."

Fanner Sobolo fingered a crooked nose, his red-rimmed eyes thoughtful.

His nose hadn't been crooked six months ago. It had been broken by Hap Kingman's fist, when the gunman, killing mad with whiskey, had tried to shoot up a fiesta dance in the schoolhouse.

It had been Hap Kingman who had braved the drunk's guns and had beaten him to a raw, trembling hulk in the hand-to-hand combat which had followed.

Russ Melrose knew that Sobolo had not forgotten that incident. He knew that Sobolo had sworn revenge. He had seen Fanner Sobolo at Kingman's trial, and knew that Sobolo had paid for drinks on the house the evening after

Kingman had been sentenced to death by a Del Rio judge.

"Kingman is over in the hoose-gow now," grunted Melrose. "I just came from there. And Kingman says he thinks the customs authorities will give him a new trial. That being the case, his prior conviction may not hold water. Kingman's liable to get off without losin' any skin from his neck, after all."

Fanner Sobolo turned to the bar, seized his glass of redeye, and downed it. Then, wiping his mouth with the back of a hairy hand, Sobolo snarled out:

"I say the dirty skunk ought to be lynched. An' damned if I ain't ready to tie the hang knot!"

The lawyer hooked thumbs in armpits and smirked at the saloon toughs gathered about him.

"Talking about a lynching bee is easy, Fanner. But I doubt if any man in this town has guts enough to see a hanging through. And it takes a lot of men to yank a prisoner out of jail and string him up. I got my doubts, Fanner, about you being able to muster up enough men to lynch Kingman—not that he doesn't deserve lynching."

Fanner Sobolo bristled at this challenge. His whiskey-inflamed mind was far more reckless than was usual in the man who made no bones about the fact that his triggerless guns were for hire.

"Yeah?" bellowed the lobo. "How about it,

men? Are we goin' to sit tight an' see Hap Kingman beat the rope? Is Hap Kingman going to
draw a prison term for smugglin'?"

The barroom resounded to the hoarse calls of
Cain from the drunken crowd of riffraff. Russ
Melrose knew that lynch mobs needed only
a leader to start them on a jailward march, and
he knew that Fanner Sobolo wielded a savage
influence over the barflies who congregated in
the Purple Hawk.

"I'll furnish the rope to swing that son!" bawled
a drink-thickened voice in the crowd. "What are
we waitin' for, Fanner?"

Sobolo gulped down another shot of redeye,
and slapped his chest like a gorilla.

"Let's go, *compañeros*! This town's been
sp'ilin' for a hangin', an' nothin' would please me
more than to see Hap Kingman doin' an air jig!"

Russ Melrose grinned excitedly as he saw the
slab-muscled killer stride toward the batwing
doors, his ugly crowd of saloon hangers-on
trooping behind him.

Lynch fever was quick to spread through a
mob, and the Purple Hawk's gang of hoodlums
was in a receptive mood. Towns had been shot up
on far less provocation than Fanner Sobolo was
now offering.

A coil of rope looped over one forearm, Fanner
Sobolo strode out into the night and headed for
the nearby jail.

Two minutes later, Sobolo had presented himself at the door of Sheriff Reynolds' office, to find the sheriff gone and the jail being guarded by Grandpa Neeley, a scrawny old jailer in his middle seventies, who was too old for regular duty.

"What's this?" piped Neeley, opening the door in response to Sobolo's knock and quaking inwardly as he scanned the sea of upturned faces outside. "What you want, Fanner?"

Sobolo snarled a livid oath.

"You got Hap Kingman roostin' inside. We're after him."

The veteran jailer turned white. He had bucked lynch mobs before, and he knew the fever for murder which was burning in the hearts of the mob massed in front of the jail.

"Tell that to the sheriff, Fanner," quavered the jailer, dropping a scrawny hand to the holstered gun at his side. "Bob Reynolds is over at the coroner's office. Seems as though he's dug up evidence that Kingman ain't guilty o' Siebert's murder, and—"

Sobolo shot out a hand to clamp a skin-crushing grip on the jailer's gun arm.

"Kingman is a dirty, low-down smuggler. He wears Señor Giboso's collar. An' we intend to see justice done—an' save the border patrol the cost o' convictin' the skunk!"

Before Grandpa Neeley could make an outcry,

his head was rocked on his shoulders by a vicious uppercut from the hand of the mammoth saloon brawler.

Flinging the unconscious jailer to one side, Fanner Sobolo strode into the sheriff's office.

A ring of keys was on Reynolds' desk, near the chair where Neeley had been sitting.

The yelling mob jammed into the office as their leader, laughing like a berserk maniac, unlocked the cell-lock door and strode into the jail proper.

One of his saloon henchmen carried in the office lamp, and by its flickering beams Sobolo made out the form of Hap Kingman seated in a cell, smoking a cigarette.

The cowboy's eyes narrowed as he saw Fanner Sobolo unlocking his jail door and swinging it wide.

Standing wide-legged in the doorway, the lobo glared down at the lone prisoner on the cot.

"Say yore prayers, Kingman. You're headin' for hang rope. An' while you're thinkin' things over, try to remember how you bashed my nose into a pulp at the fiesta last fall. Remember?"

The cigarette dropped from Kingman's lips as he stood, shoulders crouched defensively.

He saw the hatred glowing in Sobolo's piggish eyes, saw the grating teeth through the screen of the saloon tough's reddish mat of beard.

Then Kingman launched himself at the

towering gunman, fists pummeling before him.

Sobolo reeled back under the unexpected ferocity of the cowboy's charge.

But yelling renegades pounced wolflike on Hap, even as he launched damaging haymakers at Sobolo's ugly visage. A moment later he was being smothered under a welter of bodies, iron-muscled fingers gripping his arms and legs.

Then, struggling dazedly, Hap Kingman felt himself being carried bodily out of the jail.

"We'll use the hangman's tree at the plaza, boys!" sang out Fanner Sobolo, as they gained the middle of the street. "An' we'll leave his carcass hangin' there as a warnin' to other snakes who may be workin' for Señor Giboso!"

The lynch mob took up the hoarse chant of hate, as they dragged their struggling victim through the night-shrouded streets toward the gnarled cottonwood at the village square where other men had died in the past.

As is the case with most lynch mobs, the real reason for their frenzy was hazy in every mind. A shrewd brain might have realized that Fanner Sobolo was carrying out a thirst for personal revenge against a private enemy. But the charge of "smuggler!" was the peg on which they were hanging the excuse for their lawless action.

As they approached the plaza, a sombreroed man rushed out of Dr. Hanson's coroner's office, and the yelling lynchers came to a halt as they found themselves faced by the grim-faced sheriff of Yaqui County, Bob Reynolds.

"What's this, Sobolo?" came the lawman's steely voice, in the death-hush which jelled the saloon mob. "Who's this you—Kingman!"

The sheriff hauled a gun from holster as he recognized the bruised and bleeding figure of Hap Kingman, supported by two of the Purple Hawk barroom crowd.

"We're swingin' Kingman, an' you ain't stoppin' us, Sheriff!" roared Fanner Sobolo, advancing toward the sheriff with murderous calm. "Stand aside!"

Liquor had given Sobolo false courage, but the leveled gun in the sheriff's hand had cowed the mob.

Hap Kingman felt the iron grasps of his captors wavering, as the sheriff's rasping voice carried to the rearmost man in the tense mob:

"There hasn't been a hangin' bee in Mexitex since I took office, Sobolo, and we're not startin' now. Kingman will be dealt with accordin' to due process of law. Get your claws up, Sobolo. You're under arrest—for incitin' mob violence!"

Hap Kingman's heart leaped with hope. In that moment, Sheriff Bob Reynolds had won. The forces of law and order had overcome the murderous insanity that gripped the mob.

Fanner Sobolo's jaw dropped. His tense hands started to waver—and then, from somewhere out of the night, came a flying rock, hurled by a drunken lyncher.

It was a lucky throw. Unprepared for attack from an unexpected quarter, the sheriff caught the full force of the flung rock, and wilted as blood gushed from an ugly welt on his forehead.

Sobolo turned to wave at his mob.

"Come on, gang! What are we waitin' for?"

Hap Kingman groaned with despair as he felt himself hauled brutally to the foot of the grim hang tree at the edge of the Mexitex plaza.

While Fanner Sobolo was adjusting a hangman's noose about Hap's neck and his henchmen were tying his arms behind his back preparatory for the hanging, other members of the mob brought a backless chair from a nearby saloon porch.

The end of the hang rope was thrown over a gnarled limb of the cottonwood and then Kingman was boosted up on the chair. The rope was drawn taut, nearly strangling the cowboy as he stood helplessly above the surging mob.

The rope was knotted about the scarred bole of the cottonwood. Then the mob shoved back to form a tight ring of hate about the doomed cowboy, as Fanner Sobolo, his face purple with fiendish excitement, stationed himself alongside the chair on which Kingman stood.

"I'm kickin' this chair out from under you, Kingman!" screamed the berserk killer. "An' if any o' Señor Giboso's men are watchin' tonight, let this be a lesson to all smugglers!"

Over on the elevated porch of a nearby gambling hall, Lawyer Russ Melrose grinned to himself as he saw the drunken mob leader draw back a booted foot to kick the chair out from under Hap Kingman, a move which would snap the cowboy's neck and plunge him into eternity.

13

HELP ON HORSEBACK

THE crash of a fast-triggered gun and the whip-cracks of bullets speeding past his head caused Fanner Sobolo to freeze in the act of kicking the chair from under Hap Kingman's feet.

Hap Kingman, from his elevated position above the mob leader, was the first to see the five hard-spurring riders who were galloping their horses into the outskirts of the hang mob.

He caught the brief winks of gun flame from the oncoming riders as they charged the mob, their horses' flailing hoofs knocking men sprawling.

Fanner Sobolo went into a killer's crouch as his right hand whipped a gun from a holster, even as an aisle spread apart the yowling lynch mob and the approaching horsemen dashed their mounts into the cleared-off circle around Kingman's chair.

Sobolo's left hand swept in a fanning motion over his prong-shaped gun hammer in the fanning technique which had served the red-whiskered outlaw in so many close-range brawls in the past.

But a pair of six-guns blazed in Sobolo's very

face as the riders reined their jouncing mounts to a halt in the form of a rough ring about the would-be lynch victim, and Fanner Sobolo crumpled under tunneling slugs without knowing from what quarter aid had come to the doomed cowboy.

Hap Kingman was dimly aware of one of the riders leaning from saddle, felt the tug of the hang rope about his throat as a knife slashed the hempen strands.

Then the rider spurred behind him, stooping low to slash asunder the ropes which were knotted about his wrists.

Pandemonium rose as the lynch mob surged back before the grim menace of guns in the hands of the other four riders. Steel-shod hoofs trampled the bleeding corpse of the ringleader as Sobolo was ground into the dirt, his gun spewing smoke.

Over on the gambling hall porch, Russ Melrose had a gun half drawn from leather before he realized that he must take no public part in the lynching bee which he had launched like a tidal wave upon the helpless cowboy.

With his eardrums stunned by the crash of sound about him, Hap Kingman leaped from the backless chair to a position astride the horse of the rider who had cut his hang rope.

He thrust a free arm about the rider's midriff to seize the saddlehorn, even as he felt the horse rear and then level out into a hard gallop under the rider's roweling spurs.

Wind tugged at the cowboy's face, whipped the short length of hang rope about his neck as he loosened the noose and hurled it aside, then clamped his knees hard against the barrel of the mustang and concentrated on maintaining his seat behind the cantle.

Long chestnut hair bannered from his rescuer's head and brushed his face, but Hap Kingman did not realize the significance of that long hair until later.

Now, he was dimly aware of the fact that they were galloping madly out of the lynch mob, heading into the outer darkness of the town plaza.

Behind them, his rescue party was galloping on its leader's heels.

Gradually the roar of the disgruntled hang mob died in his ears, was finally lost in the thunder of racing hoofbeats as the quintet of riders headed out into the sagebrush flats, putting Mexitex far behind them.

A mile from town the riders wheeled to the right and sped in the direction of his own Flying K spread.

Over ridge tops and through murky valleys, they galloped until their horses were spent with the gruelling effort. But not until they had gained the top of a ridge which commanded a view of the distant cow town and the blacker line of the Rio Grande did they rein up.

Not until he had slid from horse and turned to face the five riders did Hap Kingman realize that the men who had snatched him from the very brink of doom were all wearing bandannas pulled up about their faces.

The possibility flashed through Kingman's brain that these were members of Señor Giboso's gang of smugglers, who were coming to the rescue of a fellow member.

Peering through the starlit darkness Hap Kingman stared hard at the figure of the leader, behind whom he had ridden on the wild burst for freedom.

It was not Everett Kingman as he had suspected. Nor was it any member of Sheriff Reynolds' staff of deputies.

"I . . . I sure owe my neck to you hombres," Kingman panted, his chest heaving. "I still don't see how . . . how things happened. They happened too quick to figger out."

The sombreroed men dismounted, and one by one lowered the masking bandannas. In the darkness, Kingman recognized none of them, but he did make out that they were not Mexicans. They appeared to be ordinary American cowboys.

If so, why should they have risked a murder-hungry saloon mob, to snatch him from under the hangman's tree?

Only when their leader pulled the bandanna mask off to reveal a white, indistinct face did Hap Kingman get an inkling of the truth.

For that leader was a girl!

"Anna Siebert!" the rescued cowboy gasped. "How come—"

The daughter of the murdered Triangle S owner shook back her long chestnut tresses.

"I was at the coroner's office tonight with my foremen and three of my syndicate riders, talking to the sheriff about you," said the girl in a heavy voice. "We saw Bob Reynolds try to stop that mob."

Kingman eyed the silent men about him with bewilderment.

"But you . . . you felt like mobbin' me yourselves, durin' the trial!" said the puzzled cowboy. "And now—"

Anna Siebert, gripping the reins of her blowing horse, stared bleakly at the man she had rescued as she explained:

"There was nothing we could do but get on our horses and do what we could to get you away from Sobolo's gang."

One of the men beside her took a six-gun from holster and spun the cylinder with a quick motion of his wrist.

"I had the satisfaction of salivatin' that drunken gunhawk, anyhow," he said with a note of satisfaction in his voice.

Anna Siebert put a hand on her cowhand's arm.

"We'll all forget you said that, Elmer," said the girl. "I don't know if the sheriff will ever find out who it was who broke up that saloon mob. But one thing certain—we don't want you being arrested for Sobolo's killing, Elmer."

A weighty silence fell upon the group.

"Then . . . I take it . . . you figured I didn't kill your father, Anna," faltered Hap Kingman. "Otherwise you . . . you wouldn't have done this tonight."

The girl avoided his grateful gaze.

"After you broke jail I found evidence that you didn't kill Daddy," she said in a low voice. "He was ambushed with a rifle from on top of Manzanita Hill. I located footprints—and the ejected cartridge. Then I had the bullet removed from Daddy's body. It was a .30-30 bullet. So that proved your Colt didn't fire the shot that killed Dad."

A great burden seemed to roll off the cowboy's heart, as he realized that he stood acquitted of murder by this sad-faced girl who stood to suffer most from George Siebert's death.

With an impulsive movement, the cowboy reached out to seize the girl's hand in his own. A moment later he stood abashed, stung to the quick by the girl's snatching her hand from his grasp, her lips curling with revulsion.

"You didn't kill Daddy," she said in a taut

voice, "but that was only by a quirk of fate. You came out to the ranch with the confessed intention of killing him."

Elmer, the Triangle S rider who had acknowledged slaying Fanner Sobolo, turned to the girl and inquired brusquely:

"What are we goin' to do with this jasper, Miss Siebert? If you want, me an' the boys can take him back to town an' turn him over to the sheriff."

Kingman was aware of the fact that the other cowboys had guns out of leather, that he was hemmed in by hostile men. But his senses were too dulled from the beating of Sobolo's gang to worry much now.

"Bob Reynolds told us tonight that you are a member of Señor Giboso's gang," said Anna Siebert, turning to Kingman. "I can't think of anything lower than a smuggler of narcotics. But—I'm willing to give you a chance, Hap Kingman. On one condition."

The cowboy stared groundward, his heart heavy.

"I'd promise you anything, Miss Siebert," whispered the cowboy. "I owe you my life. I'll do anything in return. Only—I'm not really a smuggler. I give you my word on that."

Anna Siebert thrust her bridle reins into the cowboy's hand.

"Take my pony," she said. "He's fast, and has

143

plenty of bottom. By daylight you ought to be far out in the Sierra Secos."

Muttered words of dissent came from the Triangle S riders.

"You mean," stammered the puncher she had called Elmer, "that you're turnin' this smuggler loose, boss?"

The girl lifted her chin defiantly.

"He gave me his word he didn't work for Señor Giboso."

The Triangle S cowman snorted his contempt.

"Beggin' your pardon, Miss Siebert, but you bein' a woman, you're apt to overlook the pizen meanness of Hap Kingman. The sheriff caught Hap with dope in his possession. He told us at the coroner's office that Hap admitted he got that dope from Señor Giboso."

Kingman interrupted eagerly:

"If I could talk with you alone, Miss Siebert, I could tell you my story. You could turn me back to Bob Reynolds if you didn't believe it."

Anna Siebert turned away, a tumult of emotions making her tremble in the darkness.

"I'm giving you my horse," she whispered brokenly, "on the one condition that you promise to get out of Texas—forever." She whirled to face him. "Would you promise me that?"

Knots of muscle gritted on Kingman's jaws. He was aware of the sullen hostility of the Triangle S riders, but he knew they were under her authority.

"I promise to hightail it out of Texas for keeps, Miss Siebert!" he vowed solemnly. "Soon as I get the money I'll send it to you for this bronc and saddle. And I'll thank you till the day I—"

The girl moved away, pushing through the silent men about her.

"Straddle that pony and ride, Hap!" she told him. "Ride—before I come to my senses and send you back to the sheriff!"

For a moment Hap Kingman paused. Then, looping the bridle reins over the horse's head, he wedged boot toe in stirrup, gripped the horn and swung aboard the leggy pony that had carried him away from the menace of the cow town.

"Adios, Miss Siebert!" called the cowboy, spurring away from the horsemen. "I won't be forgettin' what you've done tonight."

The little knot of Triangle S riders swore under their breath as Hap Kingman spurred the girl's pony into a gallop, and vanished into the encircling darkness of the Texas night.

When the sound of hoofbeats had ebbed and died away, Elmer turned to the grim-faced girl at his side and said respectfully:

"Miss Siebert, you know that us boys would do anything you say. We proved that when we choused that Kingman feller away from Sobolo's crowd tonight. But damned if it wasn't hard work keepin' my gun holstered when you let Kingman make a gitaway."

Anna Siebert inhaled deeply.

"A woman's got intuition about things, Elmer," she whispered wearily. "Somehow away from here, I think Hap Kingman can make good. He's got a man's heart, given the chance. I don't think I made a mistake."

14

ON THE DODGE

THE Texas sun dawned over the Big Bend country to find Hap Kingman hidden in a rocky draw far back in the Sierra Seco range.

But he was only temporarily safe; he knew that. Sheriff Bob Reynolds, perhaps backed by the border patrol, would undoubtedly start combing the badlands for him with posses.

In a manner of speaking, his name had been cleared of the charge of murdering George Siebert—if the startling news which Anna Siebert had divulged could be construed as an acquittal.

"Some dry-gulcher was squattin' on the brow of Manzanita Hill when I was talkin' to Siebert," thought Kingman, trying to puzzle it out. "Somebody with a carbine, probably, accordin' to what Anna said about the coroner diggin' a .30-30 slug out of Siebert's brisket."

Siebert's murder was no accident. Kingman could not bring himself to any conclusion but that the ambusher had known that Kingman's visit to the Triangle S outfit had been for the purpose of forcing a showdown with the syndicate boss.

But who would want Siebert killed?

The key to the riddle lay in the answer to that question, Kingman knew.

Was it one of Siebert's cowhands? That seemed unlikely, for Siebert had a local reputation for being popular with his men. After all, the Mexitex Land & Cattle Syndicate paid top wages to its range riders. So far as Kingman knew, Siebert had no personal enemies.

Bitterness against Siebert no longer burned in the cowboy's heart, despite the memories he had carried since earliest boyhood of a red-masked hombre who had shot his father and mother in cold blood eighteen years before.

It had come as a distinct surprise when the lawyer, Russ Melrose, had informed him that his father's slayer was George Siebert, the respectable cattleman. Yet Russ Melrose would have no reason to lie about the identity of—

"Russ Melrose!" cried the cowboy aloud. "He knew I was aimin' to kill Siebert. He could have ridden out to the Triangle S ahead of me, and watched me arguin' with Siebert there on the Triangle S porch. Then he saw Anna comin' around the corner, maybe, and knew her appearance would bust up the shootout I was hoorawin' her dad into, so Melrose could have killed Siebert with a long-range rifle—"

No, it didn't add up. It didn't make sense.

Melrose was an influential citizen of Yaqui County; hardly a man with guts enough to plot a murder. Besides, Melrose had nothing to gain from Siebert's murder that Kingman could figure out.

"I've promised Anna Siebert I'd hightail it to other parts, so I can't very well stick around and try to solve this mystery," the cowpuncher muttered. "I better be thinkin' about savin' my hide instead of restorin' my reputation."

He stationed himself in a prickly pear thicket on the crest of a Sierra Seco foothill, a vantage point that gave him a wide view of the terrain below. In the far distance he could see the greenish line that marked the Rio Grande.

Mexitex was hidden beyond the hazy skyline to the southwest. But if any posse moved in the middle distance, Hap knew his eagle-keen eyes would pick up a telltale column of dust, in plenty of time to mount the pony Anna Siebert had given him.

Hunger gnawed at his vitals. He had located water in the draw where the pony was hobbled, but food was unavailable. He had no weapons, so that it was impossible to get a rabbit or deer.

By nightfall, he had figured out a plan of action. Back at his Flying K ranchhouse he had money, blankets, food supplies. He doubted if Sheriff Reynolds would post a guard at the ranch, for it was against all likelihood that the fugitive cowpuncher would dare come back to his own ranch.

There would be guns and ammunition available at his home ranchhouse, too. Thus outfitted, he would be in a position to make his break for freedom. Luck had already enabled him to cheat the gallows and a lynching mob; he could not play it any further.

With the coming of darkness, Hap Kingman saddled his borrowed pony and rode down out of the foothills. He was familiar with every inch of the territory, and utilized this information now to avoid box canyons or open spaces where his horse's hoofs would leave a telltale track.

The stars had wheeled to the midnight position in the heavens when he neared the familiar outlines of the Flying K spread, where Sheriff Les Kingman and his wife had played out their lifetimes.

A thousand memories of his own boyhood with Everett Kingman rose to haunt the fugitive cowboy as he tied his horse in a bosque of dwarf cottonwoods a quarter mile from the Flying K ranchhouse, and proceeded on foot toward the familiar buildings.

He was glad that his kindly old foster parents had not lived to see the disgrace he had brought their proud name. It seemed impossible that the maelstrom of destiny had seized him, turned him from an industrious young ranchman to a wanted owlhooter, on the dodge for probably the balance of his lifetime.

Cautiously he approached the ranchhouse, on the alert for possible guards placed there by Sheriff Bob Reynolds on the off chance that the fugitive might try to return to his home under cover of night.

But he gained the front porch without difficulty, and after a long period of listening, dared to try the front doorknob.

It was unlocked. A moment later Hap Kingman slipped noiselessly into the house, and began feeling his way toward the bedroom where Everett Kingman slept.

The room was empty; dim starlight streaming through an open window on Everett's bed proved that.

He went to his own room, and then to the one in which Sheriff and Mrs. Kingman had used. All were empty.

"Everett's probably buckin' the tiger in some Mexitex saloon, as usual," thought Hap. "Anyhow, it's all for the best."

From a bureau drawer in his own bedroom, Hap Kingman obtained a cartridge belt and a holstered .45, a gift from his foster-father on his fifteenth birthday. He breathed easier when he had the reassuring weight of a gun buckled about his midriff.

Removing blankets from his bed, he wrapped

them in an oilskin slicker and tied them into a bedroll. Then he tiptoed to the kitchen, stopping in a corridor to obtain a pair of Sheriff Kingman's scuffed old saddlebags.

Reaching the kitchen, the cowboy was groping about in the darkness obtaining canned goods, a slab of bacon, coffee, sugar and other supplies for the long trail that stretched before him, when a soft voice startled him from out of the darkness:

"I leckon that is you, Mist' Hap?"

Hand coiled about gunstock, Hap Kingman relaxed as he recognized the oily whisper of his faithful old ranch cook, Wing Sing. The aged Chinaman had come barefoot from his own quarters in a shed off the kitchen, his sharp ears detecting the sound of someone moving in the house.

"Yeah—it's me, Wing Sing."

The two men met in the darkness, and gripped hands. Hap Kingman knew that of all men in Texas, he could trust the moonfaced old Oriental to the limit.

"I figger mebbeso you come back home, Mist' Hap," whispered the aged Chinese. "But you no ketch up sleep here. Mebbeso Mist' Reynolds fligger mebbeso you try to hide here, no?"

Hap Kingman shouldered the food-packed saddlebags and nodded in the gloom of the Flying K kitchen.

"I'm on my way now, Wing Sing. I've got some

dinero hid under the clock on the mantelpiece. I'll get that, and then vamoose. I don't reckon I'll be seein' you again, old pard, so I'm glad I woke you up tonight."

Wing Sing's sibilant voice said, "Velly solly, Mist' Hap, but the money, she gone. Mist' Everett take him money from undah clock, two-thlee day ago. But here—I bling you money."

Kingman's heart flooded with gratitude as the kindly old Chinaman pressed into his hand a roll of currency—Hap had no doubt but that it represented Wing's life savings.

"Thanks, old pard. I'll return this loan as pronto as possible. You know where Everett is?"

Wing Sing shrugged.

"No sabby where Mist' Everett is. Not in Mexitex town—me come from town tonight."

Hap rubbed his lower lip thoughtfully. Everett's absence was not hard to figure out. He was probably out in the Chihuahuan wilderness somewhere on one of Señor Giboso's smuggling jobs. The suspicion brought a stab of pain to the cowboy's heart.

"Well, adios, Wing Sing. Don't expect to hear from me for a while——and keep your lip tight-buttoned about me comin' here for guns and supplies tonight. I got to be dustin'."

The two shook hands in farewell, and unseen in the darkness tears rolled down Wing Sing's cheeks. They had been close, this orphan of

153

the rangeland and the old cook who was many thousands of miles from his own beloved China.

A moment later, Hap Kingman was striding out of the front door of the only place that he had ever known as home.

Because he had thoroughly scouted the porch, and because he had received Wing Sing's assurance that the ranch was not guarded, he was caught by surprise when a dark figure loomed out of the murk beside him and a six-gun barrel prodded him in the ribs.

Despair seized the cowboy's heart, and he slowly lifted his arms.

"All right, sheriff. I won't cause trouble."

The dark figure grunted.

"I ain't the sheriff," came the voice of his brother, Everett Kingman. "But I spotted you comin' in, Hap. I figgered you'd be back for your dinero, so I waited out by the pumphouse tonight."

Hap Kingman's relief turned to dread, at the icy tones in which Everett addressed him. Everett spoke more like a foreman than the man who had been raised alongside him as a twin brother.

"What's the bur under your saddle, Everett?" demanded the cowboy. "How come you got a gun in my ribs thisaway?"

Everett Kingman reached out to lift the Colt .45 from his brother's holster.

"If you think I'm turnin' you back to the sheriff

to collect the reward on your noggin' you're mistaken," rasped Everett Kingman. "But I'm takin' you over to the cave on the south bank o' the Rio."

Hap Kingman looked at him.

"Isn't it enough that I'm a wanted man, with the border patrol huntin' me and the sheriff postin' a reward for my capture? Why can't you let me take my chances on gettin' out of the country?"

Everett Kingman's snarl was like a beast of prey.

"I saved you from the sheriff's gallows once," he reminded Hap ominously. "You repaid that favor by double-crossin' me an' Señor Giboso."

Hap Kingman bridled angrily.

"Juan Fernandez did the double-crossin'!" he retorted hotly. "Your damned go-between in Mexitex thought more of the reward he'd get out of my carcass than he did of stickin' by the smugglin' ring he worked for."

Everett Kingman shook his head mercilessly:

"Get goin' to wherever you got your hoss cached, Hap!" he ordered, jabbing Hap's side with his gun muzzle. "Señor Giboso will be waitin' over at that cave on the Mex bank. You can tell Señor Giboso you didn't double-cross us. If he believes you, it's *muy bueno* with me. If he don't—your blood ain't on *my* conscience!"

155

15

SEÑOR GIBOSO UNMASKED

DOWN the windswept mesa toward the Rio Grande, through night thick enough to cut with a bowie, the two Kingman brothers rode.

The hot, seething tide of hate was beginning to swell in Hap Kingman's heart, as he rode his horse grimly toward the river and Mexico. Stripped from him, now, was any feeling he had ever had for the degenerate drunkard who had been raised as his brother.

"I been a damned fool," said Hap, hipping about in saddle to stare at the rock-faced outlaw who rode at his stirrup. Starlight glinted faintly off the blued-steel barrel of the six-gun which Everett Kingman held above the pommel, alert for any attempt at getaway on the part of his prisoner.

"Meanin' what?" asked Everett. "Meanin' that you shouldn't've risked comin' back to the Flyin' K? Any dodo knows that was foolish. What if Sheriff Reynolds had dabbed his loop on me, instead o' you?"

Hap quelled a fierce desire to launch himself

at the man who had shared his life as a brother during the past eighteen years.

"I mean," said Hap, "that there is such a thing as misplaced loyalty. When Fernandez turned me over to the border patrol, I could damn well have told the law what I know about you bein' a tool of that hunch-backed smuggler, Señor Giboso. But I didn't. I figgered that I owed you a debt of loyalty because you sent those greasers to get me out of jail that night."

Everett laughed, his voice harsh as a saw on a hardwood knot.

"Loyalty don't exist when you're on the dodge, *hermano*. You won't live long enough to use that info, but it's good advice. When you're an owlhooter, the only man you can trust is yourself."

They reached the rim of the mesa and slanted down into the Rio Grande's eroded channel. A few minutes later they were riding with boots straddling their saddle pommels, as their horses swam in withers-deep water through the muddy current of the Rio Grande.

They gained the Mexican bank at a point a hundred yards upstream from the towering shale bluff whose chapparral-choked base hid the entrance to Señor Giboso's cavern.

Keeping Hap under the menace of his gun, Everett ordered the cowboy to dismount. They tied their horses to a salt cedar, and then headed toward the brush which matted the base of the Chihuahuan bluff.

Everett Kingman gave a low series of whistles as they approached, a signal which was instantly answered by a cone-hatted Mexican who appeared magically out of a boulder nest as they walked by.

"Señor Giboso is waiting, amigo," grunted the sentinel. "And thees hombre ees Señor Kingman, *si*?"

The guard's slurring Mexican voice was familiar to Hap Kingman, and an instant later Everett's reply told him who the smuggler was:

"Correct. An' if things turn out like I figger they will, I wouldn't be surprised if Señor Giboso don't give you the pleasure o' chuckin' Hap's carcass to the catfish, Fernandez."

As they burrowed through the chaparral toward the cavern, Everett commented with a brittle laugh:

"That was Juan Fernandez. You spilled the beans about him bein' a smuggler, when you delivered that contraband to his hut the other night. Fernandez got boogery an' lit a shuck out o' Mexitex for fear the border patrol might put two an' two together. Juan ain't even claimin' the reward due for yore capture."

Everett gripped the cowboy's arm as they entered the black maw of the cave, and any notion Hap might have entertained to turn on his brother was discouraged by the prodding .45 muzzle in his spine.

A moment later they rounded the bend of the cave, and Hap Kingman found himself once more inside the damp-smelling smugglers' rendezvous.

Only one horse was now stabled in the underground hide-out; and seated at the rough pine table beside a kerosene lantern was the horribly deformed figure in sombrero and serape whom Hap recognized as the smuggler chief he had contacted in Maduro—Señor Giboso.

"Ah—we meet again, Señor Hap!" whispered the *contrabandisto*, drumming the pine table with gloved fingertips as Everett ushered his prisoner into the glare of the lantern.

Sweat dewed the American cowboy's face as he stared at the glittering eyes above Señor Giboso's mask. It struck him queer that the smuggler chief should wear a mask at all, here in the sanctuary of his headquarters.

"I delivered that load of dope to the man you told me to deliver it to," replied the cowpuncher evenly, as he saw Everett Kingman walk over and straddle a powder box at Señor Giboso's left elbow. Everett kept the Colt six-gun on the table in front of him. "It isn't my fault if Juan Fernandez double-crossed you when he turned me over to the border patrol along with the contraband."

For a long minute, Señor Giboso stared at the

unarmed cowpuncher before him. Hap got the uneasy sensation that he was facing a hostile judge who, with his next breath, would pronounce a death sentence. And Hap, having undergone just that experience at the Mexitex courthouse, felt the same shudder of apprehension coast down his backbone. This verdict would be one from which there would be no hope of pardon or reprieve, he knew.

"We will take up that matter in a few minutes," whispered the masked outlaw. "I was not expecting Señor Everett to capture you at all, let alone today."

The hump-backed smuggler stood up, and flung off his poncho. In doing so, he revealed a peculiar hardness about his shoulders, a set of straps which supported the burden of a peculiar packsack buckled high up on his back.

As he removed the packsack, Señor Giboso stood revealed as a hoax! His hunchback—the deformity that had given him his Mexican name— was nothing more nor less than the leathern sack he carried perched on his shoulders! A packsack which, viewed with a poncho covering it, looked like a humped spine!

Oblivious to Hap's gasp of astonishment, Señor Giboso turned to Everett Kingman and whispered hoarsely:

"Before you take this shipment to Mogollon, I've got another job for you, Everett. I'm expecting Joe Ashfield, the Triangle S foreman, to take a shortcut across the Sierra Secos on his way home from El Paso. He'll be carrying over thirty thousand dollars of syndicate money, and I want you to get that dinero for me."

Hap Kingman had not yet recovered from the shock of discovering the secret of Señor Giboso's disguise, so that the outlaw's instructions to ambush a man did not register on his brain.

"Señor Hap," went on Giboso in his sibilant whisper, "you betrayed my organization. You delivered the contraband to Señor Fernandez in a careless fashion that told outsiders that he was a smuggler. Juan was forced to protect himself by turning both you and the contraband over to the federal authorities."

Everett Kingman snarled nastily:

"The damned skunk did it on purpose, chief. He was aimin' on double-crossin' us, if you ask me. He ought to be gut-shot."

Hap Kingman was staring hard at the masked outlaw. A question was hammering at his brain: if Señor Giboso were a Mexican, as was generally supposed, how did he speak with such flawless English without a trace of peon accent?

"Men do not make mistakes when they work for Señor Giboso," went on the masked leader in his reptilian whisper. "You are going to die, Señor Kingman. And your own brother will fire the bullet that kills—"

With a yell of desperation, Hap Kingman lashed out a boot toe which landed with terrific force on the underside of the table top immediately before him.

The swift, totally unexpected move dumped Everett Kingman and Señor Giboso off their feet as the table upset, knocking the kerosene lantern and Señor Giboso's packsack to one side.

With a running leap, the cowboy pressed his momentary advantage as he saw Everett Kingman's six-gun go flying off into the murky cavern.

Even as the two smugglers struggled to throw off the table and rear to their feet, Hap Kingman launched a bone-crushing boot straight at Everett Kingman's jaw.

The kick landed flush on the point of the smuggler's chin, and Everett's bulging eyes glazed with insensibility as he flopped back.

The lantern lay smoking on its side, its wick still burning. By the guttering rays of the light, Hap Kingman rushed Señor Giboso as the latter pawed frantically for a holstered gun.

The cowboy drove a rock-hard fist at the masked face of Señor Giboso, saw the blow send the smuggler reeling to crash up hard against the limestone wall of the underground chamber.

Señor Giboso's ball-tasseled Mexican sombrero went flying as he crashed against the cavern wall, and as the hat fell to the ground the blue bandanna mask dropped away to reveal Señor Giboso's hate-twisted visage.

Even as Hap Kingman locked his fingers about Señor Giboso's right arm to prevent the outlaw from drawing his .45 Colt, he stared into the crook's face and recognition made him gasp Señor Giboso's real name:

"Russ Melrose!"

16

BOOT-SOLE HUNCH

RUSS MELROSE brought up his left knee in a jarring blow to Kingman's solar plexus that left him limp. But with bulldog tenacity the cowboy kept his grip on the lawyer's gun wrist, hanging there with all his weight as he fought to prevent the exposed "Señor Giboso" from triggering a slug through him.

Their rolling legs kicked the lantern to one side, but it continued flickering and smoking.

With a supreme effort, Melrose wrested his Colt out of leather, but a flesh-crushing pressure of Kingman's hand made him drop the gun before he could flex his trigger finger.

Frantically, Kingman kicked the six-gun far back into the shadows.

Then the two separated and struggled to their feet, lungs heaving with labored breaths as they squared off, fists raised, eyes hunting for an opening.

Melrose opened his mouth to scream for help to Juan Fernandez, the Mexican guard outside the cavern. But before he could give voice to the yell, Hap Kingman rushed him with berserk fury.

A rib snapped under Kingman's terrific punches, but the Mexitex lawyer was a big man. His slabby muscles held the power of a grizzly, and he matched Kingman, reach and weight.

Both men were fighting for their lives, and they knew it. If Kingman got across a punch that would drop Melrose, the lawyer knew he would be dragged forthwith to the Yaqui County sheriff, and his grim secret exposed.

The cowboy, on the other hand, knew just as surely that the smuggler would never allow him to leave this subterranean rendezvous alive, if he gained the upper hand in their conflict.

They swept into a grapple, Melrose's talonlike fingers clawing at the puncher's throat, fingernails razoring ribbons of flesh from his Adam's apple. But, before the throttling pressure of those fingers could close about his windpipe, Kingman had pounded his way into the clear with blows which reduced the lawyer's beaklike nose to a squirting pulp, sealed up one eye and brought blood to a battered lip.

Everett Kingman could not come to his chief's aid; the treacherous gringo lay sprawled as he had fallen, knocked out by his brother's kick to the jaw in the initial onslaught.

Breaking through the lawyer's desperate defense, Kingman drove a pile-driver right into the lawyer's plowshare jaw.

The punch carried every ounce of the cowboy's wiry, supple weight behind it, and staggered the lawyer.

Breathing hard through grating teeth, Hap Kingman pounced with tigerish ferocity to follow up his advantage.

Toe to toe they slugged for a brief moment, and then the lawyer crumpled to his knees, arms lifted defensively to shield his head.

But a jarring series of rights hammered against an exposed temple, and with a gusting sigh of agony, Russ Melrose collapsed on his side, eyes glazed with the stunned look of a pole-axed steer.

Panting heavily, Hap Kingman hunted in the murk until he found the lawyer's six-gun.

Then he righted the smoking lantern and made his way to where the lawyer was pulling himself into a sitting position, blood dribbling through his splayed fingers as he lifted both palms to his beef-steaked face.

"A lot . . . o' things . . . are a damned sight . . . clearer to me . . . now, Melrose," gasped Kingman, training the muzzle of the Peacemaker at the groaning lawyer below him. "I can see now why you wore a mask an' whispered. You didn't want even yore men to know that Señor Giboso was the lawyer who ramrods the Mexitex court. You didn't trust even Everett—"

Hate blazed behind the film of pain in Melrose's eyes as he stared at the black bore of a gun in Kingman's hand. Melrose was a hard man as well as evil. No trace of cowardice was in his bearing, now that he knew his life hinged on the trigger finger of Kingman's hand.

"You won't get out of here alive, Kingman!" wheezed Melrose thickly. "Fernandez isn't the only greaser guarding this cave. There are four or five men scattered up and down the Rio bank."

Kingman grinned crookedly.

"You're not in any position to bluff me, Melrose!" snarled the cowboy. "You're the hostage that'll see to it that you and me cross the Rio Grande in safety. If Fernandez takes a shot at me in the dark, I'll kill you first."

Kingman stared down at the lawyer's boots, and a sudden hunch dawned in his brain.

"You baited me into goin' out to kill Siebert—you didn't have to turn my father's six-gun legacy over to me, if you hadn't wanted me to kill Siebert that day," the cowboy said bitterly. "What was the idea, Melrose? Why did you want George Siebert out of the way?"

The lawyer fingered a rapidly closing eye.

"It was your idea, Kingman. You were getting revenge because Siebert shot your mother and father. I just did my duty—like I promised Dev Hewett before he died. The rest was up to you."

Kingman continued staring fixedly at the lawyer's hobnailed boot soles.

"Anna Siebert found boot tracks in the dried

mud up on top of Manzanita Hill, Melrose," said the cowboy at length. "She got the coroner to dig out the bullet that killed Siebert. It was a steel-jacketed .30-30 slug."

Kingman thought he saw Melrose go pale under the impact of this information.

"What's that got to do with me?" challenged Melrose, getting shakily to his feet. "You tryin' to pin Siebert's killin' onto me, Kingman?"

The cowboy grinned mirthlessly, his thumb caressing the knurled prong of the .45 he held leveled on Melrose's chest.

"Wouldn't it be interestin'," he suggested, "if those boots of yours matched the tracks in that dry adobe on Manzanita Hill? That'd prove you shot Siebert."

"Didn't I defend you in court?"

"Defended me! You let yourself give enough testimony about me and that six-gun of my father's to hang me, and you know it."

Russ Melrose shook his head defiantly.

"You won't pin any killing onto me, Hap. It'll be my word against yours. You're a wanted killer. A smuggler—"

Kingman laughed harshly.

"A smuggler, railroaded into workin' one night for Señor Giboso. An' who is Señor Giboso? None other than Russ Melrose, who'd ride down to Maduro town whenever he did a smugglin' job. Wait till Sheriff Reynolds and the border patrol hear *that*—and we'll see how far your bogus respectability gets you with a jury. And Everett will squeal on you to save his hide—"

Catching the angry cowboy off guard, Russ Melrose opened his bruised mouth and bawled at the top of his lungs:

"Fernandez! Pedro! Help—"

The yell echoed deafeningly in the stuffy confines of the cavern, and for an instant Kingman was tempted to blast a .45 slug into the lawyer's belly.

Instead, he leaped forward and clubbed the six-gun barrel hard across the lawyer's head, wilting him in an inert heap at the cowboy's feet.

Spinning about, Hap Kingman heard Mexicans shouting to each other outside the cavern, confirming Melrose's threat that Juan Fernandez was not the only smuggler guard outside.

The yells got closer, telling the trapped cowboy that Señor Giboso's sentries were sprinting toward the cavern to determine the cause of their leader's frantic cry for help.

Stooping swiftly, Hap Kingman jerked at the lawyer's left boot until it came off Melrose's leg.

Then he sprang to the lantern and smashed it, plunging the cavern into darkness.

He was not a moment too soon. Running feet slogged into the entrance of the cavern, and hoarse Mexican voices called to their leader inside.

Feeling his way along the curving wall of the underground chamber, Hap Kingman crept to the opening of the cavern.

A moment later he heard three Mexicans grope past him, spur chains clanking.

"A light!" came Juan Fernandez's frightened whisper. "Strike a match, Pedro. Something is wrong."

Taking advantage of the Mexicans' confusion, Hap Kingman slipped behind them and felt his way along the cave until the natural tunnel took its right-turn bend toward the Rio Grande outside.

A match flicked inside the cave, but Kingman was already outside. Against heavy odds, he knew it would have been impossible to attempt holding Everett and Señor Giboso prisoners.

The quick reinforcement of the lawyer's Mexican guards had turned the tables on Hap Kingman. But outside would be his waiting horse.

He forced his way through the brambles until he came to two horses, those belonging to himself and Everett, where Juan Fernandez had tied them to a dwarf cottonwood.

Swiftly he swung into saddle and spurred Anna Siebert's pony out into the river.

Behind him, hoarse yells came from Fernandez and his fellow Mexicans as they discovered the unconscious bodies of Everett Kingman and the

171

gringo lawyer they had known as Señor Giboso, their smuggling chief.

Shots shattered the quiet of the night, as the Mexicans opened fire on the dimly visible form of horse and rider, now out in midcurrent.

Bullets spat geysers of muddy water about Kingman's swimming horse. A slug plucked his sombrero brim. Others ricocheted off the river, whined off into the night.

Then the winking gun flashes ceased, as Flap Kingman made good his getaway to the black background of the Texas bank.

17

TRACKS ON MANZANITA HILL

THE Sierra Seco range, looming sinister and forbidding against an eastern horizon that was beginning to pale before the advent of a lifting sun, was known to be the refuge of hunted men throughout southwestern Texas.

Hap Kingman spurred his horse in that direction now, thankful that he had gained a fair knowledge of the trackless mountains during his youthful hunting trips after deer and mountain lions.

He could never go back to Mexico, he knew. Although he stood cleared of George Siebert's actual murder, he was still a hunted man, wanted for jail break, and for complicity with a smuggling ring.

Furthermore, he had given Anna Siebert his oath to leave Texas. But, from some remote point, he intended to ship back to her by Wells Fargo express a package which would contain the boot he had shucked from Russ Melrose's leg tonight.

If the hobnails in the sole of that boot matched the ambusher's tracks the girl had found on Manzanita Hill, overlooking her father's Triangle S ranchhouse, it would give her something tangible to provide Sheriff Bob Reynolds.

And that lawman, cagy man hunter that he was, would sooner or later spy out Russ Melrose and capture him in the role of Señor Giboso. When that day came, perhaps destiny would provide a way for Hap Kingman to come back to the only range he had ever known.

But until then he was an outcast, and if he valued his hide, he would steer far and clear of Mexitex for many moons to come.

As the blanket of night lifted slowly and the crags which spiked the Texas horizon began to wear edges of gold and rose light, the cowboy made out landmarks. Mexitex town, a sprawling blot miles to the west, along the Rio Grande. A tiny speck on the terrain that marked his own Flying K home. And nearer at hand, between the Flying K and the ridge where stood his mount, were the whitewashed walls of George Siebert's Triangle S.

Only two miles beyond and below him, he could see the small ridge named Manzanita Hill because of the profusion of the red-barked scrub which carpeted its slopes.

The cowboy's gaze dropped to the Coffeyville boot tied to his saddlehorn—the hob-nailed footgear belonging to lawyer Russ Melrose. Then his vision focused on the brushy crest of

Manzanita Hill, where an unknown dry-gulcher had fired a bullet into George Siebert's chest.

"I'll settle my curiosity first-hand!" decided the cowboy, reining about and spurring toward the Triangle S ranch buildings. "This early, I'm not likely to be spotted."

He rode ridge tops, scanning the surrounding country sharply for riders who might be in the saddle at this hour.

The rising sun threw his long shadow before him as he reached the base of Manzanita Hill, the bulk of the ridge hiding any view of Siebert's ranch.

Picketing his pony carefully in a brush-choked draw, Hap Kingman tucked Melrose's boot under his elbow and climbed to the summit of the ridge.

He paused a moment, looking down at the north porch of Siebert's ranchhouse. Distinct in the ruddy glow of the Texas dawn, the cowboy saw the spot where he had encountered the syndicate boss in his wheelchair on that grim afternoon of showdown.

Kingman's heart began racing with suspense as he worked his way along the ridge, eyes searching the ground for the telltale clues to ambush which Anna Siebert had told him about the night before.

Then, at a point where a buckthorn thicket formed a hedge directly overlooking the spot where George Siebert had died, Hap Kingman discovered the tracks which Anna Siebert had hunted out before him. The tracks which told the girl that Hap Kingman had not slain her father— clues which had directly been responsible for Hap's being alive today.

The rains which had soaked Manzanita Hill had turned the adobe to thick gray mire. Anyone walking in that mud would leave clear and distinct tracks which the succeeding sun would harden into an imperishable record, like casts made of plaster of Paris.

"It was Melrose. No doubt of it!"

Kingman muttered the words, as he knelt to examine a series of hob-nailed tracks which had hardened in the mud behind the buckthorn bush.

Carefully, the cowboy fitted Russ Melrose's boot into the tracks. They fitted exactly, to the last tiny variation of the pattern of the hobnails on the soles.

A strange torrent of emotions swept through the outcast puncher, as he tried to absorb the knowledge which this evidence proved. Placed in the capable hands of Sheriff Bob Reynolds—

"But Melrose is a slippery snake. He's been a lawyer too long to let circumstantial evidence swing him. He'd say he bought those boots from somebody, or that they were stolen and returned at the time of Siebert's murder. He'd wiggle out some way or other."

A rustling in the brush before him made Kingman leap to his feet, hand sliding to his holstered gun.

Then he froze, as he saw Anna Siebert standing before him, bareheaded in the morning sunlight.

"So it's you, Hap," the girl said heavily. "I saw someone moving around up here, from my window. But I . . . I hardly expected . . . to find you."

Hap Kingman fumbled clumsily with his Stetson brim. For the moment, all thought of embarrassment or dread of being discovered by Anna Siebert was erased in the sheer beauty of the girl before him.

The ruddy sunlight did something to her face, highlighting the straight nose and firm mouth, her warm hazel eyes.

She was wearing a fringed buckskin blouse this morning, bright with Indian beadwork. Her split skirt was likewise of buckskin, and she was wearing taffy-colored riding boots.

"I thought you gave me your word to leave Texas yesterday," Anna Siebert went on, as he stood there in silence. "Why do you persist in—"

Hap Kingman stepped forward, gripping Melrose's boot in his hands. Words tumbled from his lips as he blurted out:

"Miss Siebert, I meant it when I promised to vamoose. But things have happened durin' the night. Things you'll find it hard to believe. I know who murdered your dad, now, and framed me with that killin'. This is his boot."

Anna Siebert listened slowly with melting disbelief as Hap Kingman told her of his capture by his brother Everett the night before at his Flying K ranchhouse, his visit to Señor Giboso's cave on the Mexican side of the Rio Grande, and the startling discovery he had made regarding Señor Giboso's true identity.

"And then his boot—it proves beyond a shadow of a doubt, Miss Siebert, that Russ Melrose is the ambusher we're lookin' for. Not only is Russ Melrose masqueradin' as Señor Giboso, on the south side of the border—but for some reason, he wanted your dad put out of the way."

The girl's lips curled in a scornful smile.

"And you were the man he chose to . . . to put Dad out of the way."

Kingman's heart sank as he saw the grim light of tragedy in the girl's eyes. Although technically he had not murdered George Siebert, he knew that Anna still regarded him as a potential killer, and would never forgive him for the murder mission that had brought him to the Triangle S.

"Miss Siebert," pleaded the cowboy, "you can't understand. That memory I had of an hombre murderin' my parents—well, it poisoned my heart, made me brood all through my boyhood years. When Russ Melrose told me who I was— that my father, Dev Hewett, wanted me to avenge

178

his death—I guess I sort of went loco. It sounds flat to say, but I don't . . . I don't think I would really have prodded your dad into a shootout. My temper would have cooled—"

Unexpectedly, Anna Siebert stepped forward and thrust out a hand to grip the cowboy's.

"Hap, let us forget the unfortunate past. The thing to do now is to see what we can do about Melrose."

Anna Siebert walked with him down the other slope of Manzanita Hill and conducted him into the big living room of the Triangle S ranchhouse, where a crackling fire cut the morning chill.

"You may be mystified as to what motive Russ Melrose would have in wanting my father dead, Hap," she told him, after giving orders to a wide-eyed *mestizo* to serve them breakfast immediately. "But I know—or at least, I think I do."

Sombrero on his knee, Hap leaned forward as the two sat down before a cowhide-covered table by the fireplace.

"You know why Melrose shot your dad?"

"Yes. I found out, while going through my papers last night, that my father owed Melrose ten thousand dollars. I knew he mortgaged the syndicate last year when blackleg wiped out our herds, but I didn't know Melrose held the paper."

Kingman's jaw dropped as understanding flooded his brain.

"Then if Melrose can foreclose that mortgage—"

"He could be in control of the Mexitex Cattle & Land Syndicate, Hap," finished the girl.

Kingman whistled to himself.

"When is that mortgage money due Melrose?"

"It's due," the girl replied, "one week from today."

"And I don't suppose," Kingman said anxiously, "that you got that much money floatin' around to pay Melrose off?"

To Kingman's relief, Anna nodded.

"Yes, thank God. On the day your trial ended, Hap, our syndicate trail herd reached El Paso. The stock was auctioned off for top prices. By now my foreman, Joe Ashfield, will be riding back to Mexitex with more than enough to pay off Melrose."

Kingman started to grin with relief. Then he sat up with a jerk. For the first time since his grim fight with Señor Giboso, he recalled the murder plan which the smuggler had outlined to Everett Kingman.

"Holy smoke," groaned the cowboy, his face blanching. "Anna, I got terrible news. Melrose is plannin' to waylay Joe Ashfield and get that dinero. I heard him tell Everett that—"

The girl went white as Kingman told her briefly that Señor Giboso had instructed Everett to do so.

Despite the grim light which this turn of events placed on Anna's future, the two devoured the breakfast which a *mestizo* served them.

They were still eating when a knock at the front door brought the Mexican servant shuffling into the room. He opened the door to reveal a towering figure on the threshold.

"Bob Reynolds!" cried Anna Siebert, as the rawboned sheriff from Mexitex removed his Stetson and strode inside. "You've—"

Reynolds' glance shot from Anna Siebert to her guest at the breakfast table. Then his arm plummeted to his side and came up with a long-barreled Peacemaker.

18

DEPUTY'S BADGE

HAP had leaped to his feet at the sheriff's entrance. He stood now, weak and tense, arms climbing ceilingward before Reynolds' drop.

"I came out to question you about who it was who saved Hap Kingman from that lynch mob last night," said Reynolds, "but I see the answer before me. I suspected as much."

Hap saw Anna Siebert step swiftly between the two, but he made no move to take advantage of her being in the line of fire.

Reynolds shoved her aside as he took a pair of handcuffs from his chaps pocket.

"No, Bob—don't arrest him till you've heard from me."

The mustached lawman paused a moment, eyes alert for a treacherous move from Hap Kingman.

"Anna girl," he said finally, "I was the hombre who went for Doc Hanson the night you was brung into the world. I was the hombre who told George that your mother had passed on, bringin' you into the world. We've always been amigos, you an' me. But you can't ask me not to arrest an escaped prisoner."

"You'll be glad not to arrest him when you've heard us out, Bob," she said pleadingly. "Take his gun, but don't handcuff him."

She stood aside as the sheriff extended a hand toward Hap Kingman.

"Hand me yore smokepole butt first, kid," said the sheriff. "An' no spooky moves."

Hap Kingman removed gun from holster and handed it, stock foremost, to the sheriff. The latter's brows arched in amazement as he read the name "Russell Melrose" engraved on the ornate ivory handle of the Colt.

"How'd you git the lawyer's shootin' iron, Hap?" he queried. "Has he been out here?"

The three of them sat down. Before either Anna or Hap could speak, the sheriff thrust Kingman's gun into the waistband of his chaps and said to the girl:

"Was it you an' your Triangle S riders who killed Fanner Sobolo an' rescued Hap last night?"

"Yes. We saw you get rocked by that mob. There wasn't anything else to do but save Hap, if we could."

The sheriff chuckled.

"You'd made yore getaway an' the lynch mob was mysteriously vanished from the plaza by the time Dan Kendelhardt woke up an' put a plaster on my sore noggin." Reynolds grinned. "Well,

184

you say you got somethin' to tell me. If it's to clear Hap of killin' George, I'll believe that. But don't forget that the U. S. Customs men are still holdin' a smugglin' charge on him."

Anna Siebert seated herself in front of the old lawman and outlined in crisp detail the startling narrative which Hap had told her concerning Russ Melrose's dual life.

There was a long silence after the sheriff had finished inspecting Melrose's hob-nailed boot, as he tried to comprehend the bewildering mess of evidence Hap Kingman had unearthed.

"This takes my breath, sort of," he said. "I reckon there's no use ridin' down to the Rio to check on Hap's story, because Señor Giboso an' Everett have no doubt flew the coop. But—even if Melrose has the gall to show up in Mexitex again—we haven't anything to really jail him on. Not yet."

He reached to his side and handed Hap Kingman the lawyer's revolver. With a grateful smile, the cowboy replaced it in his holster. He knew it was a vote of confidence from Reynolds.

"The thing that disturbs me the most," Reynolds went on, "is what Hap said about Señor Giboso orderin' Everett to ambush Joe Ashfield an' get that syndicate dinero. If Melrose gets that money, he'll be able to take over your syndicate."

The girl nodded broodingly. As the heiress to the murdered syndicate boss, the affairs of the big range organization weighed heavily upon her.

"I wouldn't be surprised if Melrose carries through his scheme to ambush Ashfield," the sheriff continued. "Tell me this—will your foreman be accompanied by all your riders? If he is, Everett wouldn't dare try to ambush him."

Terror came into Anna Siebert's eyes.

"That's just it, Bob!" she cried. "Joe will be riding alone, over the Sierra Seco short cut from the Marfa stagecoach road. My other cowboys are picking up a herd of feeders at Fort Luego and won't get back to the ranch for another couple of weeks."

The sheriff and Hap Kingman exchanged worried glances.

"Ashfield won't be expectin' trouble," muttered the sheriff.

He paused a minute, thinking. Then he looked up quickly.

"Anna, if I remember right, your men always bed down at the Drover's Hotel in Marfa, on their way home. Is that right?"

"Yes. They always have."

"Then here's what I'm going to do. I'm going to send Hap up to Marfa, to warn Ashfield about Melrose's plan."

Kingman nodded approval.

"I figger you've still got time to get to Marfa, and wait at the Drover's Hotel until Joe Ashfield shows up there," said the sheriff. "Once forewarned, Joe can get through O.K. He an' you can travel by night across the Sierra Secos where Everett would be holed up."

"Or Melrose might abandon the whole idea, knowing that Hap overheard his orders to Everett," suggested Anna Siebert.

The sheriff waggled his head.

"Wish I could think so, Anna, but we can't afford to risk it. Not with the whole syndicate at stake, an' Melrose holdin' trumps."

Sheriff Reynolds fumbled in a pocket of his chaps and produced a nickel-plated star, which he handed to Kingman.

The latter turned it over curiously. "What's this for?" Kingman asked, puzzled.

"An hour ago I was all fixed to hogtie you an' take you back to the calaboose, Hap." The lawman grinned. "Now I'm offerin' you a job as special deputy, to ride to Marfa an' be Joe Ashfield's bodyguard on the return trip. How about it?"

Hap thrust the emblem of frontier law into his pocket, and stood up. His heart thumped with a warm new thrill as he shook hands with the man who had once been cast in the role of hangman with Hap as his victim.

"I'll see Ashfield through hell an' back, Sheriff. When do I start?"

"Now. You got a horse outside, I take it?"

"On the far side of Manzanita Hill. With *alforjas* all packed an' ready."

"Good. I got another gun out in my saddlebags for you."

Anna Siebert bade the new deputy good-bye at the door, and watched the two men as they walked out to the sheriff's horse, tied to the hitch rack beyond the low wall of the yard.

As Reynolds handed Hap the .45 Frontier Colt which he had stowed in his saddlebags, the cowboy recognized it as the cedar-butted weapon which Dev Hewett had owned—the six-gun legacy which the dying outlaw had willed to his son eighteen years before—and which Reynolds had previously taken from Hap.

"Why in hell couldn't that no-account brother Everett o' yours been the whelp o' Dev Hewett?" wondered the sheriff. "Then he'd be mixed up in all this. I've always liked you, Hap. I've seen you grow up. You got good stuff in you. Sheriff Kingman would be proud of you."

Hap Kingman scowled, as a new thought occurred to him.

"Here's hopin' nobody in Marfa figgers I'm a desperado on the dodge, and prevents me from seein' Ashfield when he gets to that hotel. Mebbe you better give me a note to show people you really made me a deputy, Reynolds."

The sheriff rummaged in a saddlebag and produced a sheet of paper, on which he scribbled a brief statement and signed it. As he folded the sheet and handed it to Kingman, the cowboy recognized it as one of the hundreds of posters distributed through Yaqui County offering a reward for his own capture.

Then, with a final handshake for good luck, Hap Kingman strode off up Manzanita Hill to get his horse and get started for the cow town of Marfa.

Anna Siebert joined the sheriff as the latter prepared to leave.

"We've only got Melrose's word for it that Dev Hewett *was* Hap's father," she told the sheriff. "Do you suppose anyone in Mexitex knows the details of how Les Kingman happened to adopt Hap and his other brother?"

Mounting, the sheriff looked down at her.

"Only the doctor who attended Hap's mother when she died of gunshot wounds. Harry Hanson."

"And Dr. Hanson is still missing?"

"Haven't seen hide nor hair of him since the day before Hap's trial was ended. Darned if it doesn't smell peculiar. Ain't like the coroner to just up an' disappear thataway."

Hap Kingman rode into the cow town of Marfa near sundown the day following his departure from Siebert's ranch.

He had no particular worry about meeting the Triangle S foreman, Joe Ashfield, or the other syndicate trail drovers who were homeward bound. He had a speaking acquaintance with

189

Ashfield, having been a Flying K rep on cattle drives where Ashfield acted as trail boss.

At the time of Kingman's twenty-first birthday, when he had come with his brother Everett to Russ Melrose's office, there to hear their foster-mother's will and to learn the startling disclosure regarding his own ancestry, Joe Ashfield had been nearing El Paso, hazing the syndicate beef to railhead.

This meant that Ashfield knew nothing of the tangled events which had transpired in Mexitex during his absence. It would even come as a shock to Ashfield to know that his boss, George Siebert, was dead. By the same token, Ashfield would not know of Kingman's murder trial and subsequent adventures with the law.

Arriving in Marfa, Hap turned his Triangle S pony over to a livery barn for grooming and graining. The first thing he saw was a placard tacked among others on the livery-barn wall—a reward poster mailed to the Marfa sheriff by Bob Reynolds, for the capture of Hap Kingman, dead or alive.

Being a stranger in Marfa, however, the cowboy had little cause to worry. In the event some person recognized him and summoned the Marfa sheriff, it would be a simple matter to present Bob Reynolds' letter of introduction, and to produce the deputy sheriff's badge which proved he was no longer riding outside the law.

He went first to the Drover's Hotel, a rambling frame building patronized by stockmen. There he engaged a room, after making inquiries which informed him that Joe Ashfield had not as yet arrived in Marfa on his return trip from El Paso.

Then Hap visited a barber, to get rid of that quarter inch of beard which stubbled his chin.

A good meal followed—the first real one in several days.

Then he returned to the Drover's Hotel, prepared to wait until the returning ranch foreman passed through Marfa. As the cow town was the only settlement between El Paso and Mexitex, Kingman knew there was little likelihood of his missing the homeward-bound Triangle S foreman.

He had not long to wait. The next evening a knock sounded at his door and he found the lanky, red-headed trail boss of George Siebert's ranch standing in the corridor outside.

"*Como 'sta*, Hap," greeted the foreman, shaking hands. "The ramrod o' this hotel tipped me off that you been here roostin' until I showed up."

"That's right, Joe," answered Kingman, pulling up a chair for the trail-weary foreman. "I got bad news for you."

Carefully withholding all details of his own connection with the case, Kingman informed the Triangle S foreman of Siebert's murder.

"Poor Anna," was Ashfield's first reaction to the shocking news of his boss' death. "This'll be tough on her. She's all alone, now, an' runnin' the syndicate is a man's job."

Kingman reached in his pocket and drew forth the deputy's star.

"Bob Reynolds figured you needed a bodyguard, Joe." The cowboy grinned. "Not that you couldn't take care of yourself, but you had no way of knowin' your life may be in danger on this trip back to the home spread."

Ashfield looked startled. "My life in danger? How come?"

"You're carryin' over ten thousand dollars with you—money belongin' to the syndicate. At least, ten thousand is the Triangle S cut of the beef herd you just auctioned in El Paso. And the hombre who killed Siebert is liable to want to glom his mitts onto that dinero, in order to prevent Anna from payin' off that mortgage."

Ashfield leaped to his feet.

"You mean that turkey-necked lawyer, Russ Melrose, would try to ambush me? He's the one who holds Triangle S paper!"

Hap nodded.

"Can't go into details, but that's how things stack up."

Ashfield unbuttoned his shirt to expose a leathern money belt strapped about his middle.

"Closer to thirty thousand bucks o' syndicate

dinero I'm packin'," he whispered hoarsely. "An' me not even dreamin' that I might get myself ambushed."

Ashfield grinned, and stuck out a hand.

"I ain't takin' offense at you bein' sent along to guard me like as if I was a tenderfoot, Hap." He chuckled. "Startin' in the mornin', I reckon me an' you ride together. An' if Anna hasn't done it already, I'm thankin' you for riskin' yore hide to ride along with me."

Next morning, by prior arrangement, the two breakfasted before sunrise in a Chinese restaurant on Marfa's main street. By daylight they were both in saddle and heading southward on the stagecoach road to Presidio.

By midafternoon they left the protection of the well traveled road and headed in a short cut across the Sierra Seco mountains in the direction of Mexitex.

Hap Kingman maintained a steady silence regarding Russ Melrose, not knowing how much he could speak without betraying the sheriff's confidence. Kingman knew that Joe Ashfield was a trustworthy man, a cowpoke who had been with George Siebert for over twenty years. But the more he entered into explanations, the more likelihood of revealing his own part in things.

The thirteen notches, on the .45 Colt heirloom which he carried, took on a sinister implication to the puncher. A notched gun butt was the mark of a wanton killer, a man who boasted of his victims.

Such a man had been Dev Hewett.

"Plenty o' hoodlums roamin' wild in this part o' the Sierra Secos, Hap," commented Joe Ashfield, as the Triangle S foreman threw out an arm to encompass the upflung badlands about them. "Reckon it might be a wise idea to separate a little bit. I'll go on ahead, an' you stay enough behind so that if we're jumped by ambushers, we wouldn't git cut down together."

Hap Kingman's eyes ranged about the boulder piles and cactus clumps on all sides of them—a veritable paradise for an ambushed gunman to hide in—and agreed that the foreman's pre-caution would be wise.

Two men, riding close together, would offer a much better target than if they separated by some trail.

Accordingly, Joe Ashfield spurred on ahead. They were following a little-used game trail which snaked off through the Sierra Secos and would cut many miles off their trek.

Hap Kingman, his eyes trained to eagle keen-ness by his many hunting trips into these desolate uplands, scanned the surrounding malpais con-stantly.

During past years, Joe Ashfield had always returned to the home ranch by this route. If Russ Melrose had any ambush intentions, therefore, attack would occur somewhere along this trail; of that Kingman was positive.

For miles they rode, sparing their horses, hands on gun butts, nerves and wits alert for a smudge of dust or a moving dot on the landscape which would indicate the presence of another rider in the area.

The westerning sun forced the men to lower their Stetson brims, and made the job of keeping a lookout difficult.

Hap Kingman, holding his forearm up to shield his vision against the oblique rays of the sun, suddenly stiffened in saddle as he saw a tiny puff of smoke issue from an ocotillo cactus clump midway up a slope whose base they were skirting.

He opened his mouth to yell a warning to Ashfield, riding fifty yards in advance, but the words froze in the cowboy's throat as he saw the Triangle S foreman suddenly pitch up his arms and topple sidewise in the saddle.

At the same instant there was wafted to Kingman's ears the sharp, flat report of a high-calibered rifle.

Spurring off the trail toward the shelter of a nearby outcrop of granite, Hap Kingman saw a second and third puff of smoke issue from the ambusher's hide-out up the hillside.

Close on the heels of the whiplike sound of the gunshots, he saw Joe Ashfield's body twitch under the impact of tunneling slugs.

A dry feeling was in Kingman's mouth as he saw the Triangle S foreman pitch out of saddle, his sombrero tumbling off as his head hit the ground.

And then Kingman was appalled to see that Ashfield's right boot, twisting in the stirrup as he fell, had become entangled in the tapadero.

Ashfield's horse, panic-stricken by the clatter of shots and feeling the jerk on its reins as Ashfield tumbled from saddle, suddenly reared and headed off along the trail at a mad gallop.

Kingman saw Ashfield's body jouncing along the stony ground, like a sack of spuds towed at rope's end.

"And here I am without a long gun!"

Kingman muttered an oath as he peered over the top of his sheltering granite outcrop, then ducked as a .30-30 bullet sprayed gravel in his face. The ambusher was gunning at him!

Crouched in shelter, Kingman saw Joe Ashfield's leg finally knocked free of the stirrup. But there was no hope that the syndicate trail boss could still be alive.

Even if Ashfield had escaped death from the three bullets which had struck his body, Kingman knew that the man's skull had undoubtedly been crushed as he was dragged along the rocky ground. And his mount's steel-shod rear hoofs had no doubt hammered the trailing body, as well.

Dismounting, Hap Kingman gripped his bridle reins in one hand as he hurried to the far edge of the granite outcrop where he had taken refuge against the dry-gulcher hidden on the slope above.

As he did so, he caught sight of the ambusher scuttling along the hillside toward a nearby gully, his body bent almost double as he left the cactus thicket.

Swiftly Kingman triggered two shots at the running hombre, saw his bullets kick up dust far short of his target. A moment later the killer had vanished into the draw.

19

LONG-RANGE DUEL

THERE was a .45-70 Winchester carbine in the scabbard of Joe Ashfield's saddle, but it might as well have been on a distant planet.

Even as Hap Kingman watched he saw the foreman's horse, its saddle stirrups flapping wildly, vanish over a boulder-cluttered ridge a half mile distant.

Ashfield's body had not moved since it had broken free of the ox-bow stirrup that had trapped the Triangle S rider. It now lay, crumpled grotesquely, at the end of a settling pall of dust which marked the skidding path of doom.

"If I try to reach Joe's body and get that money belt, that ambusher will pot me," Kingman thought, wiping sweat from his face. "And it won't do any good for me to wait for him to ride down to Ashfield's body, because that's out of six-gun range."

Even as he spoke, Kingman saw the ambusher ride out of shelter of the low-rimmed coulee, mounted on a leggy roan mustang.

At two hundred yards, the cowboy could not

tell who the ambusher was. He wore a Mexican sombrero, and a Mexican serape bannered in the wind as the ambusher spurred his horse wearily down the slope. He did not believe the ambusher was Everett Kingman.

"If it's Melrose, he's still wearin' his Señor Giboso costume," decided Kingman. "But it's probably one of Melrose's gunhawks, that he sent up here in wait for Joe."

The Mexican-clad killer was obviously heading down the hill toward Ashfield's corpse. Sunlight glinted redly off the barrel of a rifle which the ambusher kept in readiness.

"This skunk knows I haven't a rifle, or I'd've used it when I had the chance," thought Kingman, climbing back aboard his pony. "At this rate, all I can do is sit here and watch while that skunk robs Ashfield and rides off."

Halfway down the hill toward the trail, the sombreroed killer dismounted and knelt beside a boulder to rest the rifle barrel across it.

In the nick of time, Kingman realized that the dry-gulcher was intending to drive him to cover, for the lobo had now ridden far enough down the slope to catch sight of the cowboy who had ridden under the lip of the granite outcrop.

Even as Kingman reined his horse about and spurred for the protection of the outcrop's eastern end, the ambusher's rifle spat harshly and a .30-30 spanged on the rocks alongside Kingman.

The single shot had its intended effect; it drove the helpless cowboy around the corner of the rock.

When Kingman was out of sight, the rifleman proceeded down to the trail on foot, leading the roan behind him at rein's length. Reaching the trail, the outlaw strolled calmly to where Joe Ashfield's corpse lay sprawled in the rubble.

Hap Kingman groaned aloud. He could not leave his horse and take a chance on running from bush to rock and thus get within six-gun range of the ambusher who was coolly preparing to rob Ashfield's corpse.

To do that would be to risk being trapped in the open, and Kingman had already seen the ambusher's uncanny skill with a rifle.

Peering around the granite ledge, the cowboy cursed with impotent fury as he saw the serape-clad desperado jerk out the tails of Ashfield's shirt, going unerringly to the currency-stuffed money belt which the Triangle S foreman wore.

"Thirty thousand bucks, and me helpless to defend it!" moaned the cowhand, gripping his cedar-butted Colt in an agony of impatience. "And worse than that, Anna Siebert will lose her ranch if I don't get that dinero back!"

Even as he looked, Hap Kingman saw the killer stand up, the money belt dangling from his fist like some manner of snake. The ambusher rolled up the belt and tucked it under his armpit, then calmly tightened the girth of his saddle and remounted.

Then, with a taunting wave in Kingman's direction, the robber spurred off toward the southwest, following the trail to Mexitex town.

Knowing that it would be suicidal to venture into the open so long as the outlaw remained in effective rifle range, Hap Kingman waited with mounting impatience until the killer topped the skyline of the next ridge and dipped from sight.

"He may hole up and try shootin' at me when I come out in the open," decided Kingman, remounting. "But my hoss can outrun his, if it comes to that."

The cowboy spurred into a gallop, drawing rein alongside Joe Ashfield's body.

If he had any hopes of finding a spark of life left in the unfortunate foreman of the Triangle S, that hope was blasted.

Ashfield's skull was split open from some jagged rock he had been dragged over. The leg which had become wedged in the stirrup was twisted, obviously broken.

Further than that, blood leaked from three bullet holes in the foreman's chest. Any of them would have proved fatal. Kingman doubted if Ashfield had been alive when he had toppled from saddle. He probably never knew what hit him.

"No time to bury you, old pard," panted Kingman, untying his own bedroll and covering

Ashfield's corpse with a blanket. "Best I can do is try and tally your killer and get that dinero back. With darkness only an hour away, it seems that ambusher is going to win this pot."

Kingman left the trail, making a wide circuit along the southern base of the ridge beyond which the ambusher had vanished. He knew that to continue on the trail would bring an inevitable bullet, and he did not intend to share Ashfield's grisly fate.

Rounding the shoulder of the ridge, Kingman caught sight of the ambusher, a half mile away. Sure enough, the outlaw had halted as soon as he had topped the rise, waiting in case the cowboy rode in pursuit.

Then a moving object off to the left attracted Kingman's eye, and a low cry blew from his lips as he recognized Joe Ashfield's saddle horse a short distance away.

The foreman's mount had been attracted to a mountain bench sparsely stubbled with gramma grass, and was now grazing, the sun glinting off the polished seat of the empty saddle.

This was a stroke of luck. There was the .45-70 rifle in Ashfield's saddle scabbard, if it had not dislodged during the horse's wild gallop to freedom.

Unbuckling the coiled riata at his pommel, Hap Kingman shook out a loop as he spurred toward the dead man's horse.

The bronc threw up its hammer head and sniffed as Kingman approached, riding at a wild gallop.

Then Ashfield's horse bolted, but trailing bridle reins made the animal stumble and Kingman quickly overhauled the riderless mustang.

He kept an eye on the mounted killer up the ridge, as he closed in on Ashfield's horse with lariat whirling in air. He heard the far-off crash of gunfire, heard the high-pitched whine of bullets overhead as the ambusher sought to get his range.

But a running target was hard to hit, and a moment later Hap Kingman's loop settled about the horse's neck and he was snubbing the rope to his saddlehorn.

Leaving his trained peg pony, Hap hurried along the rope until he could seize the horse's bit ring.

He grinned with relief as he saw Ashfield's heavy carbine still intact in its scabbard. And hanging from the saddlehorn was a brown leather case containing a pair of field glasses.

The cowboy paused long enough to strip the horse of saddle and bridle and turn it loose. Then, uncasing the binoculars, Kingman squatted down and focused the glasses on the figure of the ambusher.

The latter had stopped shooting and was riding along the trail, as if uncertain whether to ride closer and open fire again on his target.

"Melrose!" gasped Kingman, as the high magnification of Ashfield's glasses revealed the crooked lawyer, seemingly close enough to touch. "Even if you get back to Mexitex, you'll swing for ambushin' Joe!"

The high-powered field glasses showed Kingman every detail of the Mexitex lawyer's hate-twisted visage. The lawyer at the moment was busy reloading the magazine of his Winchester, from cartridges contained in a Mexican-style bandolier slung across his chest.

Dropping the glasses, Hap Kingman pulled Ashfield's rifle from its boot, wound up his rope, and climbed back on his horse.

"Now we're on an even footin'," rasped the cowboy, as he spurred grimly in Melrose's direction. "In fact, my rifle will outshoot yours."

They were a thousand yards apart, now. Kingman had shot more than one mountain goat or elusive deer at that range, but the idea of hunting for a fellow human was a strange sensation.

He had never killed a man, but no restraint or revulsion was in the cowboy now as he spurred grimly toward showdown. If his marksmanship proved equal to putting a .45-70 bullet through Russ Melrose, he would feel triumph instead of regret.

Less than an hour of daylight remained, and Melrose had every chance of taking flight. A getaway would be easy.

But, strangely enough, the Mexitex lawyer was showing no signs of turning tail and making his escape from the approaching cowboy.

"He realizes I got him spotted, now," decided Kingman, as he saw Russ Melrose fling off the Mexican serape to give his arms freedom. "I've called him, and it's a showdown."

When he had cut the distance between them in half, Hap Kingman drew rein and levered a shell into the breech of Ashfield's rifle.

Melrose sat his horse, motionless on the trail at the top of the ridge. The hillside was barren; there were no coulees where Melrose could hide himself, let alone his horse. The rocky soil was even devoid of a boulder or a mesquite bush where Melrose could hole up.

The reason for the lawyer's choosing shoot-out instead of flight was obvious. So long as Hap Kingman was alive, and knew that Melrose had ambushed Joe Ashfield and robbed his dead body, then Melrose could not return to Mexitex and take over Anna Siebert's cattle syndicate.

Grimly, the lawyer leveled his Winchester carbine at the halted cowboy down the slope. Even as he pulled trigger, he saw Kingman's rifle flash.

Smoke cleared away from both guns, and the two long-range duelists saw that their opening shots had both missed their marks.

Then they spurred closer, each reloading their rifles as they maneuvered toward each other for a shootout which inevitably would bring death to one or both.

20

BUZZARD BAIT

HAP saw the lawyer rein up his horse and jump suddenly from saddle.

Ground-tied, the horse remained motionless as Russ Melrose ran a dozen yards to one side and put his mount out of the line of fire.

But the Flying K cowpuncher chose to remain in saddle, believing that he presented a more difficult target on a moving horse than on the ground.

Cagily, Russ Melrose did a running dive toward the ground as Kingman triggered two fast shots at the lawyer. The .45-70 bullets kicked up spurts of sand behind Melrose's heels.

Belly down to the ground, Russ Melrose propped up his smoking Winchester with one elbow, his gunsights following the cowboy as Kingman broke into a gallop, making a wide circle to put the gray background of the mountains behind him.

Melrose's next bullet was desperately close, but Kingman knew the odds against being hit were in his favor. In all probability, Melrose would soon have to reload his rifle magazine, and in that moment when he had his enemy at a disadvantage Kingman intended to strike from closer range, where his unfamiliarity with the strange firearm would not count against him.

And then Russ Melrose changed tactics.

Disregarding the mounted cowboy who was keeping in constant motion, Melrose drew careful aim at Kingman's fast-moving horse.

The animal, broadside to the prone lawyer, was as good a target as a deer—and Melrose had reason to be proud of his marksmanship.

A yell of dismay wrenched from Hap Kingman's lips as he felt his pony rear aloft on its hind legs, its body jolted by the impact of a .30-30 missile which struck it through the withers and shattered its spine.

With a high-pitched neigh of agony, the Triangle S pony pitched groundward.

Desperately trying to kick boots from stirrups, Kingman felt the pony's legs buckle, felt the horse pitch sidewise.

A red wave of pain shot through Kingman as his right leg was pinned between the horse's barrel and the rocky ground. Even as the horse kicked violently in its death throes, the cowboy heard the grisly snap of his shin bone fracturing under the pressure of the horse's weight.

Darkness swirled about Hap Kingman and he fought doggedly to fight off unconsciousness.

Fireworks spun before his vision; he became aware of the fact that he was pinioned to the earth with twelve hundred pounds of horseflesh on his broken leg.

His face gleaming with the sweat of sheer agony, Hap Kingman reached around for the rifle which he suddenly realized was no longer in his grasp. It lay on the ground well out of reach.

Then Hap's senses skidded over the edge into oblivion.

Russ Melrose leaped to his feet with a yell of triumph and raced for his horse. He levered a shell into the firing chamber of his Winchester as he spurred down the slope toward the trapped body of his victim.

Melrose approached warily, lest Kingman might be luring him into six-gun range with a ruse of unconsciousness.

But the cowboy made no move as Melrose approached from the rear. Kingman's arms were outflung, and his weight was resting on one holstered gun. Before Kingman could possibly draw his other .45 Colt, Melrose could shoot.

Dismounting, the lawyer approached the fallen horse and rider, and made certain that Kingman was knocked cold.

Melrose pressed the muzzle of his rifle against the back of Kingman's head, but then he seemed to change his mind. He squatted down to remove the uppermost Colt from the cowboy's holster, noticing with relief that it was his own gun which Hap Kingman had taken from him in the Rio Grande cavern.

Lifting Kingman's weight, the lawyer tugged the other six-gun from its scabbard. It was Dev Hewett's six-gun legacy to his son, its backstrap significantly notched thirteen times.

Melrose tossed the gun aside. He had kept it in his safe for eighteen years, and nothing but evil luck had come from it.

"It'd serve you right, Kingman, if I waited for you to come to and told you how I tricked you into thinking you were Dev Hewett's whelp, instead of Warren Allen's," thought the lawyer with a sadistic grin. "But if I use my common sense, I'd salivate you and then hit the trail for Mexitex."

For a long interval Russ Melrose pondered another scheme. He seriously doubted if Hap Kingman, regaining consciousness, would be able to extricate himself from the weight of the dead cow pony. And there was a good chance that Kingman's leg had been broken by the fall.

Unbuckling the cowboy's lariat from the pommel, Melrose proceeded to lash Kingman's arms behind his back, knotting the rope securely.

"Reckon I'll leave you here for buzzard bait, cowboy!" rasped the lawyer. "Nobody passes this spot once in a blue moon. And when your bones are discovered, nobody'll blame me for this job."

Remounting his own horse, Russ Melrose spurred back up to the Mexitex trail. Five minutes later he had vanished over the next ridge, riding into the sunset.

Wracking pain brought Hap Kingman to his senses after darkness had fallen. He lay there in a stupor of numb agony, hardly able to realize that his arms had been trussed tightly behind him.

As the long hours of a cool mountain night revived him, Kingman became increasingly aware of the pain of his fractured shin bone. The crushing weight of the dead horse brought a numbness to his entire body.

Phantomlike shapes prowled about the fallen horse and rider, during the black hours before the dawn:

Timber wolves, attracted by the scent of the dead horse which held Hap Kingman prisoner, helpless on the cold earth, here in a forgotten corner of the desolate Sierra Secos.

Exhaustion finally overcame his pain, and Kingman slept.

The sun was several hours high when its hot, penetrating rays finally brought the doomed cowboy back to his senses.

"Looks like here is where I cash in my chips,"

thought Hap Kingman. "I'll be lucky if I'm not in hell and the coyotes nibblin' my carcass this time tomorrow!"

His frantic efforts to wriggle his broken leg from under the dead saddle pony brought only nausea and dizziness.

Awakening from one of the fainting attacks brought about by his desperate efforts to crawl free, Kingman scared away a trio of gaunt, red-necked buzzards which had swooped down out of the Texas sky to alight on the pony's stiffening legs.

As the boiling sun baked the vitality from his body, Hap Kingman became more and more feeble in his attempts to scare away the waiting, black-feathered scavengers of the malpais.

Thirst tortured him. At intervals, he raved in delirium, until his voice was lost in the raw cavern of his throat.

Finally, as midafternoon came after an eternity of time, one of the buzzards ventured to alight on Kingman's shoulder.

The puncher's swollen tongue and parched throat were incapable of screaming out the horror that seized his heart.

His spirit recoiled from the grim bird of death, but his quivering movements were not enough to frighten the buzzard.

Hap Kingman felt his sanity reeling as the bird of prey tightened its sharp talons on the muscles of his shoulder, flapped its wings with a rush of sound like a death knell.

Then the buzzard poised over Hap Kingman with cruel beak ready to rip into the cowboy's defenseless face.

21

SIERRA SECO PROSPECTOR

DIMLY, above the steady tom-tomming of blood in his eardrums, Hap Kingman heard a muffled shot.

With the crash of sound, the pain-racked cowboy was aware of the fact that the gaunt buzzard astride his shoulder had been miraculously snatched away.

Twisting his head about so that one cheek ground against the hot rubble under his head, Hap Kingman saw the black *zopilote* bouncing wildly amid a flutter of bloody feathers, a few feet away. Like a chicken beheaded on a chopping block.

Only then did the half-dazed puncher realize that it had been a bullet, smashing through the scrawny body of the bird of prey, that had knocked the buzzard to one side.

Uttering harsh squawks, the buzzard finally flopped over on its back, blood guttering from a wound that had torn through its entrails. The huge wings beat feebly, and then the buzzard relaxed, its long-clawed talons slowly opening and closing like human fingers as death relaxed tendons.

The sound of the shot filled the air with a dozen or more of the shrieking buzzards, who had been clawing at the hide of the dead horse which pinioned Hap Kingman to the ground.

Grating boots on gravel made the cowboy turn his head the opposite direction.

Physical and nervous exhaustion were bogging at the cowboy's senses, but his dimming vision made out the form of a gaunt, bony man stalking toward him, a smoking six-gun in one bony fist, a flop-eared burro following him at the end of a rope.

The hombre's shadow fell across Kingman's face, as the stranger thrust his Colt into a worn half-breed holster buckled low on a bowed thigh.

"You're in a hell of a fix, ain't you, cowboy?" greeted the newcomer, in a high-pitched voice like a clarinet with a squeaky reed. "I figgered you for daid, when I seen that turkey buzzard fixin' to tear into you. I was figgerin' to bury you."

Hap Kingman tried to find his voice, but it was impossible. He had difficulty in focusing his eyes on the stoop-shouldered old codger standing beside him.

His last conscious memory was a picture of the old-timer—a kindly face, brown as leather and adorned with a stringy waterfall mustache, under a flop-brimmed Stetson; a caved-in chest, arms with whipcord muscles, and warped legs clad in patched and faded blue Levi's.

Then all went black, as the man tried to reassure him:

"Don't worry, son. You're safe as in God's pocket, now that I've found you—"

The hombre was a prospector, as evidenced by the pickax and shovel and pair of canteens which hung on the outside of a canvas-wrapped, diamond-hitched pack on his burro.

The prospector was one-eyed, his left eye socket being a screwed-up, empty slit under a craggy brow. But the hardrock miner's left eye was blue as chipped turquoise, and it was busy.

The prospector, bred to reading sign, had no difficulty in sizing up what had happened here. And, in the habit of men who live alone in the desert with no one to talk to but themselves or their animal companions, the wizened old hombre vouchsafed his opinion to the inattentive burro:

"Gertrude, offhand I'd say this here hoss sot foot in a prairie-dawg hole an' stumbled. This here cowpoke was prob'ly dozin' in the saddle, an' got pinned down by one laig so he couldn't move."

The prospector squatted down, squinting at the horse's withers. Flies were swarming around the bullet wound which had killed the horse.

"Reckon this cowboy figgered his hoss' leg was broke, so he shot the hoss," deduced the prospector, stepping over Kingman's inert body. "That left him out o' luck, not bein' able to pull out from under the—Oh-oh!"

The oldster broke off with an oath as he saw that Hap Kingman's arms were tied behind his back.

"Gertrude, I'm thinkin' that somebody *else* must've shot this feller's hoss," he told the burro. "Now, you suppose this jasper was an outlaw? Else why'd he be tied up thisaway? Mebbe some sheriff lost him—"

With a pocketknife, the prospector cut loose Kingman's bonds. Then, salvaging the longest end of the lariat, he tied it to the horn of Kingman's saddle.

The other end of the lariat he tied to the pack-saddle of the burro.

"Now, Gertrude, it's up to you to shift that hoss' carcass so I can pull that cowboy out from under," instructed the old man. "Wouldn't be surprised ifn his laig's broke, or badly bruised. An' he's been lyin' thar two, three days mebbe."

It took the combined strength of the sturdy little jenny and the prospector's wiry muscles to shift the dead weight of the pony so that Hap Kingman's trapped leg could be freed.

The prospector made a clucking sound with his tongue as he unbuckled Kingman's chaps, slit his overall leg and inspected the discolored skin.

"Broke a bone, sure as hell," muttered the prospector soberly. "An' he's about tuckered out from thirst. Reckon he needs water, much as anything."

From his own canteen, the old desert rat sloshed a quantity of brackish water over the cowboy's head.

As soon as Kingman had revived sufficiently for the oldster to cradle his head on his lap, the prospector let him sip several swallows of water.

"That's all for now," said the desert-wise oldster. "Cain't risk you gettin' sick from overloadin' your stummick with *aqua*. First off, I got to rustle a splint an' set that laig o' yourn."

Hap Kingman was fully conscious by the time the oldster had returned from a brief hunt on the surrounding hillside, carrying with him some mesquite limbs which he had chopped off with an ax.

Dusk was falling, and the cool breeze of the desert was soothing to the cowboy's flushed temples and the raw, swollen wrists where Melrose's ropes had chafed the flesh.

"Reckon I owe my life to you, stranger," the cowboy said gratefully. "What you fixin' to do? Set my leg?"

The prospector nodded.

"Call me Allen, busky. One-eyed Allen. Lost

one lamp in a minin' accident when I was a kid, an' I been called One-eye ever since."

Allen chuckled as he saw Kingman eyeing the mesquite splints he was flattening with his knife.

"Son, if you think I can't doctor you, you're mistaken. I set my own busted laig, onct, by myself, with not even whiskey to sooth my nerves. That laig's gone too long without attention now, an' it's a two-day trip to Marfa with you the shape you're in. I got to fix that laig hyar an' now."

Merciful unconsciousness spared Hap Kingman untold agony as the fractured bone was pulled into place. When he recovered consciousness once more, it was to find that night had enveloped the badlands, and his leg was firmly bound with strips of rag and firmly splinted.

"I'm loadin' you on my burro, son," One-eye Allen told him, as he lifted the cowboy's hundred and eighty pounds with a lithe ease that belied his scrawny frame. "I got a shack over in the Sierra Secos, about ten mile from hyar. I got whiskey an' a good soft bed for yuh."

Hap Kingman had little recollection of the long night's journey back into the trackless wilderness.

Lashed with rope to Gertrude's back, the cowboy made the trip with as much comfort as he could have expected under the circumstances.

A fever had set in by the time One-eye Allen reached the tiny rock shack which he had built at the far end of a shadowy canyon, well off the faint Mexitex trail.

The cowboy was dimly aware of his benefactor lifting him off the burro, jackknifing him over one scrawny shoulder, and carrying him into the shack.

There, on a buffalo hide stretched over a straw-tick mattress, Hap Kingman lapsed into a stupor, his brow burning with fever.

After stabling his burro, One-eye Allen busied himself with necessary preparations for taking care of his patient.

He forced a few swallows of whiskey down the cowboy's throat, to fortify him against the grueling ordeal of the fever. Then, after heating water in a blackened kettle at his fireplace, Allen carefully stripped off the cowboy's clothing and bathed the puncher's chafed muscles.

It was while hanging up Kingman's shirt that One-eye Allen dropped the nickel-plated star contained in the pocket. The old prospector studied the star's inscription by lamplight, and nodded with satisfaction.

"A deputy sheriff, eh?" he grunted. "Somethin' went wrong, son, for you to have been tied up an' left to die out there on the Mexitex trail."

Covering the slumbering cowboy with a faded army blanket, One-eye Allen stretched himself out on a pile of gunny sacks on the floor, and fell asleep—

Through the following day the cowboy babbled in delirium, his fever raging.

But One-eye Allen, making a closer inspection of the puncher's injured leg, was relieved to find that no infection had set in. The fever was due to exhaustion and exposure, and one look at Kingman's splendidly muscled torso told Allen that the cowpuncher was in no immediate danger. Around midnight the fever was broken.

It was noon the second day after his removal to Allen's shack that Hap Kingman was able to partake of nourishment.

"You don't have to tell me what happened out there on the desert, Hap," said the old prospector, stoking his corncob pipe and seating himself beside the cowboy's bedside. "What happened was yore business. Only I'm glad I happened to be prospectin' in yore neighborhood. That buzzard was fixin' to spile yore face for keeps, when I drifted up to investigate."

The cowboy grinned. For the first time, his head was free of the dull, splitting ache which had accompanied the period of fever.

"I can't ever repay you for this, Allen," he said gratefully. "How long I been here?"

"Two days, Hap." The oldster lit his pipe with a coal from the fireplace, and returned to the bedside. "An' I hope you ain't in any hurry to be dustin' yonderward, son, because it'll take six weeks at least before you can walk on that laig—let alone fork a bronc."

Kingman shrugged. Waiting for a broken leg was nothing, when he realized that only by a lucky break of providence was he alive.

"So you know my name's Hap! I didn't realize I introduced myself. Was I ravin' loco durin' them two days?"

Squinting through blue tobacco smoke at the puncher, One-eye Allen shook his head.

"You didn't interdooce yoreself, Hap. I called you Hap because I figgered mebbe that was yore name."

The cowboy eyed his benefactor with sharp interest.

"But it's an unusual name," he said. "Funny you'd strike on that name to call me."

One-eye Allen chuckled.

"I've met you before, Hap. That is, if you're the man I got you ticketed for. As a matter o' fact, Hap, if I ain't mistaken, I'm related to you. I figger I'm yore uncle."

22

SECRET OF THE PAST

KINGMAN'S eyes widened in startled wonder.

"You . . . my uncle?"

The desert rat nodded, his single blue eye twinkling.

"Is yore name Allen—Hap Allen?"

The cowboy shook his head negatively. The thought struck him that this bald-headed oldster was slightly on the loco side. It was not unusual for prospectors to be lunatics. But the coincidence of Allen's having called him "Hap" was difficult to understand.

"Afraid you got me wrong, Allen. My name's Kingman. Or—as a matter of fact—my real name is Hap Hewett. My dad's name was Dev Hewett."

A look of disappointment crossed the desert rat's face.

"If yo're dead shore yore name's Hewett, then my hunch is wrong," admitted the prospector. "But you shore as hell have got Warren's hair an' eyes an' jaw."

"Warren?"

One-eye Allen puffed energetically at his pipe.

"Warren Allen. My brother. You're the spittin' image o' my brother, whom I ain't seen in nearly twenty years. Same build, same expression when you grin. As much like my brother Warren as if you was both poured into the same mold an' left to set."

Strange emotions tugged at the cowboy's heart.

"I go by the name of Hap Kingman," he said slowly, "because I was adopted by old Les Kingman, who was sheriff of Yaqui County for thirty-odd years. But I got evidence to prove that my real father was named Dev Hewett."

One-eye Allen stared out the open doorway of his shack at the heat-shimmering canyon walls opposite.

"How old are you, son?" he asked.

"Around twenty-one. I was about three years old when Mr. and Mrs. Kingman adopted me. My father and mother were killed—when I was three."

The prospector's single eye gleamed with a strange light.

"Meanin' you was orphaned about eighteen year ago?"

"That's right."

Allen turned, cocking his head as he scanned the cowboy's emaciated face in the half light of the cabin.

"Answer me one question, Hap," requested the

oldster. "Are you dead *certain* yore father was named Hewett?"

Hap Kingman started to voice his positiveness of his ancestry, and then checked himself.

He realized, with a start, that the "proof" of his birth rested solely on the word of the Mexitex lawyer, Russ Melrose. And in the light of what he now knew about Melrose, he saw that he could not necessarily accept the lawyer's word as gospel.

"Why . . . no. I . . . I'm not sure at all. The . . . lawyer who read Mrs. Kingman's will to me—he told me about my father."

Allen tapped his corncob sharply on a bony knee.

"Then you ain't a Hewett, no more than you are a Kingman. You're Warren Allen's kid—the baby son that was born to him over in San Antone, twenty-one years ago come August 10th. Nobody but Warren Allen's whelp could look as much like my brother as you do."

A far-away look came into the prospector's single eye, as he leaned back in his chair and hooked thumbs in armpits.

"I'm going to tell you a little story, Hap," began the prospector. "Twenty-one years ago, my brother Warren an' me was prospectin' in the Sierra Secos. His wife was livin' in a covered wagon, movin' wherever Warren took her—Fort Stockton, Marfa, Presidio. Their little kid was so cheerful an' gay all the time that his uncle—that's me, One-eye Allen—nicknamed him Happy. We got to callin' the little tike Hap for short."

There was silence in the little shack for a moment, a silence broken only by Gertrude's raucous bray somewhere far down in the canyon.

"Well, me an' Warren discovered a gold strike," went on One-eye Allen, his voice vibrant with a long-forgotten excitement. "It was in these Sierra Secos, somewhere. We cleaned out a small fortune in nuggets an' float ore, but we didn't have the equipment to develop the vein we discovered. It was a bonanza, though."

One-eye scratched his leathery dome to summon up almost-forgotten memories.

"Me an' Warren decided to record our claim," the oldster continued. "I headed for Fort Stockton to buy supplies, while Warren went down to Presidio, on the Rio Grande, to get his wife an' little son, Hap."

With careful detail, One-eye Allen explained that his brother Warren had drawn a map of the terrain where they had discovered their gold strike, with a red-hot nail on a strip of soft sheepskin.

"Just in case we couldn't trace our way back into the badlands and find it again—gold mines are easy to lose, in a country as big as this," Allen said. "Well, to make a long story short, I was supposed to meet Warren an' his wife Eleanor an' his kid, Hap, when they got to Marfa. But they never came back, an' I ain't seen hide nor hair of 'em to this day."

"Why didn't you go down to Presidio, if that's where your brother went to get his family?" inquired Hap.

"I did," responded the prospector. "I found out that a smallpox epidemic had busted out among the Mexicans, an' Eleanor decided to move out so Hap wouldn't catch the damned plague. She left word for Warren where she'd be, with a hotelkeeper there."

"Did your brother know where they'd gone to?"

"I reckon so. The hotelkeeper gave Eleanor's letter to my brother, when he got to Presidio an' found his family gone. But where they went to, I never found out. Nor did I get another trace of Warren."

Kingman nodded thoughtfully, following Allen's narrative with tense interest.

"And he never showed up at the gold mine?"

One-eye Allen spread his leathery palms in a Mexican gesture expressing ignorance.

"*Quien sabe*? You see, I didn't have a map, figgerin' I could never lose that claim. One reason Warren drew it was to have a map to file with the recorder. If Warren went back to the gold mine, instead of meetin' me in Marfa like he agreed, I don't know. As I said, he vanished like the earth had swallered him. An' I been huntin' that lost gold strike ever since."

Hap Kingman whistled with awe.

"You mean you never located—"

One-eye Allen chuckled at Kingman's incredulity.

"It's easy enough to lose a thing like a gold claim, out in the Sierra Secos, son." The prospector grinned ruefully. "All the ridges look alike. A man could wander a lifetime an' never cover half the arroyos an' dry creek beds. I been at it eighteen years now with nary a glimpse of the canyon we located. Mebbe I been within a stone's throw of it—*quien sabe?*"

Hap Kingman was conscious of a strange pounding in his chest, as old memories stirred there.

"This was eighteen years ago?"

"*Si*. An' now you turn up, Hap. The spittin' image o' Warren Allen. I'd stake my bottom dollar you're the son of Warren an' Eleanor. That'd make me yore uncle—not that I expect you to whoop with delight at findin' that out. I ain't worth a red cent."

Hap Kingman inhaled deeply.

"Allen," he whispered tensely, "what memories I have of my babyhood are plenty thin, by now. But my mother's name was Eleanor—that I do know. I can remember my dad callin' her that. The night they were murdered by a masked hombre. It was in Mexitex town, up the river from Presidio. That must have been where my mother went in her wagon, after that smallpox broke out."

Speaking swiftly, excitedly, Hap Kingman told One-eye Allen what little he knew of his own past—the past that lay before that unforgettable night of horror eighteen years ago, when he had been orphaned by a killer's gun.

"As soon as this busted leg is well, Allen, you an' I are headin' back to Mexitex town," vowed the cowboy. "I got a hunch we're goin to get to the bottom of what made your brother vanish off the face of the earth, why he never kept his date with you at Marfa. Things are too tangled up and complicated for me to figger out the savvy of it now, but I got a hunch we'll be able to prove that Warren Allen *was* my father—and I think I know the hombre who did the mixin' up of my destiny."

A little group of bareheaded men and women filed out of the cemetery on the outskirts of Mexitex town, situated on the crest of a bluff overlooking the sluggish Rio Grande.

Dan Kendelhardt, the deputy coroner of Yaqui County and now the only undertaker in the cow town, had just finished tamping the clods over an oblong mound of freshly dug earth.

At the head of the cemetery's latest grave was a simple granite slab bearing chiseled words:

JOSEPH ASHFIELD
Ambushed

Anna Siebert and the Triangle S cowboys had paid for Joe Ashfield's burial. Gloom had reigned throughout the rangeland ever since a posse under Bob Reynolds had returned from the Sierra Secos, bearing Ashfield's bullet-riddled corpse shrouded in an old blanket.

Ashfield had met with foul play on the little-used short-cut trail from Marfa. His horse had been found grazing with a herd of wild fuzztails many miles away, by a drifting cowpoke who had recognized the Triangle S brand and brought the saddler to Mexitex the day the sheriff returned with Ashfield's body.

Anna Siebert was the last to leave the boothill graveyard, after her Triangle S cowhands had moved off to the main street to drown their grief with liquor.

With her was Sheriff Reynolds. The old lawman put on his sombrero as they left the cemetery gate, and he took her arm as they headed toward the sheriff's home on the outskirts of town.

There, with Mrs. Reynolds bustling about to provide a noontime meal for the young mistress of the Triangle S spread, the kindly old sheriff tried to find words to comfort the girl. In Joe Ashfield, she had lost the most valuable man on her outfit.

She had counted heavily on Ashfield to help her shoulder the numerous burdens of her father's Mexitex Land & Cattle Syndicate. Now, with Ashfield dead—

"I can't see how he missed Hap Kingman," the girl said heavily. "I must send a messenger up to Marfa, Bob. Hap is probably still waiting at the Drover's Hotel, wondering why Joe doesn't show up."

The sheriff avoided Anna's gaze, and for the first time she knew that the lawman had not told her all he had found out at the time he had discovered Ashfield's mutilated corpse.

"Bob! Bob!" cried the girl, her eyes lighting with tragic dread. "Don't . . . don't tell me . . . that you found Hap's body in that ambush—"

Sheriff Kingman swallowed hard. He had dreaded this moment, but he knew the girl must know the worst.

"I . . . I got deppities investigatin' the badlands," he faltered. "But . . . I can't say for shore that Hap Kingman was dry-gulched along with yore ramrod, Anna."

The girl went white.

"Then . . . then Hap did . . . did meet Joe at the Marfa hotel?"

The sheriff inhaled deeply, and then plunged into the hard business of telling what he knew.

"Anna, I do know that Hap an' Joe were ridin' together at the time Joe was killed. But . . . I

235

haven't found Hap Kingman's body, nor any trace of it."

"Then how do you know he met Joe at Marfa?"

"The pony you loaned him, Anna. It was found about a mile away from where we found Joe's body. The hoss was almost eaten up by coyotes. There was Hap's saddle an' pack, Joe Ashfield's .45-70 rifle, an' some distance away was one of the two six-guns that Hap Kingman was packin' at the time he left us to go to Marfa."

"But no trace of Hap himself?"

Reynolds shook his head in the negative.

"It's queer as hell—er, almighty queer, Anna. Mebbe the ambusher shot Kingman's horse an' set him afoot. But why would Hap leave his guns behind?"

The girl's eyes dulled with an agony of dread.

"Melrose killed them both," she whispered huskily. "He got the money belt that Joe Ashfield was wearing—either he did, or some gunhawk Melrose hired."

The sheriff groaned his sympathy.

"We haven't got a smatterin' o' actual proof against Melrose," he pointed out. "Hap King-man is the only man livin' who can prove anything against Melrose—or that Melrose was fixin' to have Joe Ashfield ambushed so he could waylay that syndicate cattle money. But until we can locate Hap, Melrose will just laugh at us."

Anna pressed a handkerchief to her brimming eyes.

"You're sure Hap Kingman's body isn't lying out there somewhere? Could your posses have missed it?"

"A pretty slim chance, Anna. We combed that country for a mile in all directions. If Hap was lyin' dead or hurt anywhere around we'd have found him. As I say, I still got a couple deppities scoutin' the country on the off chance they may locate Hap."

They consumed Mrs. Reynolds' meal in moody silence. Anna Siebert, more than at any time since she had recovered from the shock of her father's brutal murder, felt the weight of overwhelming responsibility upon her.

Besides the crushing loss of her father and, close upon the heels of George Siebert's murder, the tragic death of her homeward-bound foreman, Anna Siebert had to worry about the theft of the thirty thousand dollars belonging to her father's syndicate.

Two-thirds of that money belonged to other ranchers belonging to the syndicate. Unless it was recovered, Yaqui County's stockmen were faced with bankruptcy.

Meal finished, Anna Siebert mounted her saddle pony and, with Sheriff Reynolds riding at her stirrup, proceeded downtown. The sheriff rounded up the Triangle S cowboys, who accompanied their boss back to the home ranch.

The afternoon of the day following Joe Ashfield's funeral, Anna Siebert was roused out of an afterlunch nap by a Mexican servant woman.

"El señor *sheriffe* ees out at the gate, señora," the *cocinera* told her. "There are other hombres weeth heem, *tambien*."

Hurriedly adjusting her hair, Anna Siebert went to the door in time to see Sheriff Bob Reynolds striding up the path, with six burly, gun-hung men clanking their spurs behind him.

Looking past her lawman friend, Anna Siebert recognized the frock-coated figure of the lawyer, Russ Melrose, with Everett Kingman at his heels. The other four men were ugly half-breeds, and strangers to the girl.

Anna's heart leaped, thinking that perhaps the strangers were deputy sheriffs and that Everett Kingman and Melrose were under arrest.

But one look at Bob Reynolds' gray, twisting face, and the girl knew that the sheriff of Yaqui County was bringing evil tidings.

"Brace up, girl," whispered the sheriff, as she stood aside to admit them into the living room of the Triangle S ranchhouse. "I'm takin' this on the chin as bad as you'll have to, Anna—even though I haven't anything personal at stake."

Anna Siebert's eyes flashed with hate as she returned Russ Melrose's insolent stare. Everett Kingman, his dissolute, haggard face twisted in a smirk of triumph, saw the lawyer flush under her stinging glance.

"I'm not so sure I want these men in my home, sheriff!" snapped the girl, her tone ringing with defiance. "In fact, Mr. Melrose, I am asking you to get out before I have the sheriff throw you out. And the same goes for that drunken sot beside you, Everett Kingman!"

Russ Melrose seated himself indolently in the chair that had been George Siebert's favorite, hooked his spurred boot heels on a table edge, and proceeded to light a cigar.

"Before you go throwing anybody out of this house, you better consult with your friend the sheriff, Miss Siebert," taunted the lawyer. "If you don't treat me more hospitably, I may be forced to throw *you* out of here. It isn't *your* home any longer."

Anna Siebert turned to the sheriff, eyes wide with concern.

"What does he mean, Bob?"

The sheriff dropped his gaze. He fumbled with trembling hands inside his chaps pocket to draw forth a legal-looking document. The paper rattled noisily in the ghastly silence of the room.

"Melrose has got the court to issue dispossession notice, Anna," whispered the sheriff, his face mottled with fury. "As sheriff, there's nothin' I can do but serve 'em."

Russ Melrose puffed twin jets of cigar smoke

through his beaklike nostrils, and laughed harshly.

"Of course, if you can pay me the sum of ten thousand dollars, plus eight months' accrued interest at six percent, those dispossession papers won't mean a thing, Miss Siebert," jeered the lawyer. "Pay that mortgage, and I get out."

The girl turned to the sheriff, a sickish feeling attacking her stomach.

"But I . . . I couldn't raise *one* thousand dollars, Bob," she told the lawman in a panicked voice. "You know that. The only money I had was in Joe Ashfield's possession, and he . . . he was ambushed by these . . . these—"

The sheriff's sharp glance made her break off. She was conscious of the fact that the four gunmen who had accompanied Melrose and Everett Kingman were fingering their six-gun butts and glancing at the lawyer, as if waiting for orders.

"The . . . the mortgage Melrose holds is several days overdue," the sheriff said huskily. "These . . . these papers here—the court has granted Melrose possession of the Triangle S ranch and the controllin' interest of the Mexitex Land & Cattle Syndicate. If you can't pay up—"

Anna Siebert controlled her mounting panic with a visible effort. A look of understanding and sympathy, mixed with helplessness, came from Sheriff Bob Reynolds.

"How . . . how soon . . . do I have to get out?"

Russ Melrose answered the question she had directed to her sheriff friend.

"Today. Pronto. From now on, Miss Siebert, I'm living here in the Triangle S *casa*. And I won't be needing your men. Rustle 'em together and have 'em pack up your personal possessions. If you aren't off this spread by sundown, my men here will help you move off."

Anna saw knots of muscle playing on the sheriff's jaws, but she saw the bleak light of defeat in Reynolds' eyes. She knew the sheriff would like nothing better than to swing into action with blazing guns.

But Russ Melrose had anticipated trouble, and had brought along his greased-lightning gunhawks to forestall any loss of temper which the sheriff might suffer, or to combat any show of resistance on the part of Anna Siebert's loyal Triangle S cowboys.

"I've figgered it out from all angles, Anna," said the Mexitex sheriff heavily. "You'll have to move out, an' surrender the syndicate books to Melrose. But yo're welcome to live at my place with Mrs. Reynolds an' me as long as you see fit."

23

HAP KINGMAN RETURNS

FORTY long, endless, dragging days had been checked off on One-eye Allen's calendar before Hap Kingman was able to move about on his injured leg. But years of clean living, plus the wholesome food and expert care of One-eye Allen, had enabled the broken shin to knit together without the danger of a lifetime of limping.

One-eye Allen had left his patient alone only once during the six weeks of his convalescence. That had been on a trip to Marfa, where Allen had purchased a mild-tempered cow pony for Hap to use when the time came for him to return to Mexitex.

On his return with the horse, Allen brought word that Hap's saddle and the .45-70 rifle, which Allen had left behind at the scene of Hap's misfortune, were no longer there.

"Some damned saddle tramp prob'ly picked 'em up," the old prospector said. "If there'd been room on Gertrude's back I'd have packed your belongin's an' that Winchester along with me that night."

Kingman shrugged.

"Forget it, unk. I can ride bareback to Mexitex, and I can pick up some artillery from friends."

One-eye Allen beamed with pleasure whenever he heard the cowpoke address him as "unk."

As Allen recalled more details of his last association with Warren Allen, Hap Kingman became more and more convinced that he, through some quirk of fate which was as yet a riddle, was really the orphaned son of Warren and Eleanor Allen.

The two were able to see hereditary resemblance between themselves, as time went on. They had the same mannerisms and skull structure and general builds—resemblances of blood relationship which were too numerous, Hap figured, to be coincidental.

But the crowning proof that they were nephew and uncle was provided by an old-time tintype photograph taken nineteen years before in San Antonio, and which One-eye Allen had among his few personal trinkets.

The tintype showed a young couple and a child of about two years. The father's picture was almost the mirrored image of Hap Kingman, differing only in the outmoded style of hairdress, the ram's horn mustache which men wore in that period.

"That's my brother Warren, an' his wife Eleanor—an' *you,* when you were knee-high to the loadin' gate of a rifle, Hap!" One-eye Allen had said. "See that cowlick on the little tike's scalp? A dead ringer for the cowlick on yore noggin."

Hap, conscious of strange, tugging emotions in his heart, had stared long and hard at the photograph of the couple he knew must have been his parents.

"I'm not doubtin' it, unk," the cowboy had said. "And just as soon as my leg is well enough for me to get around, I reckon we can find the proof we want over in Mexitex."

It was seven weeks to the day since One-eye Allen's chance discovery of the trapped cowboy—a trek which the prospector had made to investigate the focal point of soaring flocks of buzzards—that the two men set out from the prospector's stone shack, and picked up the Mexitex trail once more.

Hap was still limping, but it was due to the natural weakness of his leg muscles and not to any maladjustment of his mended shin bone. If One-eye Allen had been a doctor, his bone-setting could not have been more expert.

Two days later, when they were leaving the Sierra Secos foothills and the dim line of the Rio Grande's course was once more visible on the southwestern horizon, the two made camp at the little-known waterhole deep in the recesses of an arroyo.

"I've got a hunch that there'll be men who'll start gunnin' for me when I show up," said Hap Kingman gravely, after they had picketed their mounts and rolled up in blankets for the night.

"I been thinkin' o' that," replied One-eye Allen. "I been wonderin' if it wouldn't be a good idea for me to hole up here in camp while you look up your friend the sheriff an' see what can be done about corralin' this Russ Melrose jigger?"

Kingman pondered this suggestion for several minutes.

"*Bueno*," he said. "And if I'm not back here to report by day after tomorrow, unk, you better light a chuck to Mexitex and tell Bob Reynolds that I returned from the dead. Even if Melrose's gunnies are on the prowl, they won't recognize you as havin' any connection with me."

Feeling better for thus having an ace in the hole in the event that he ran into bad luck, Hap Kingman borrowed Allen's saddle for his own mount the next morning.

"Reckon I'll sashay over to Anna Siebert's first," he decided, "and get an idea about what's happened durin' the past two months. Then I'll get my head together with the sheriff and see what can be done about smokin' Melrose out of his den."

He spurred his pony into a trot as he approached Manzanita Hill and knew that beyond it he would find Anna Siebert's Triangle S ranchhouse. The chestnut-haired girl had been constantly in his thoughts during his long period of enforced idleness, and he had worried many times over what the loss of her syndicate money might mean to the girl.

Topping the crest of Manzanita Hill, the cowboy looked down on the red-tiled Spanish-type hacienda which had been George Siebert's home.

A number of horses were tied to the hitch rack in front of the ranchhouse yard, and the thought flashed through Kingman's head that the syndicate might be having a meeting today at Anna's home.

And then, when he was midway down the slope, he suddenly reined up with a start.

The front door of the Triangle S house opened, and two men strode out, busily engaged in conversation.

Kingman's right hand dropped to the butt of the six-gun which One-eye Allen had loaned him, as he recognized those two hombres as Russ Melrose and his foster brother, Everett.

"What in hell are they doin' here at the Tri—"

Then, like a thunderbolt out of the blue, the truth struck Hap Kingman.

Anna Siebert was no longer owner of the Triangle S. Her home now served as the headquarters of the man who had slain Joe Ashfield and stolen the cattle syndicate's money.

Failing to notice the lone cowboy midway

up Manzanita Hill, Russ Melrose and Everett Kingman disappeared from view around the white stucco walls of the ranchhouse, headed for the nearby barns and corrals.

Grimly, Hap debated whether to ride down onto the ranch grounds and force a showdown with the two outlaws. Then, realizing that the Triangle S probably swarmed with Melrose's gun-hung henchmen, the cowboy headed back over Manzanita Hill and galloped in the direction of Mexitex town.

But if Kingman believed his near-approach to Melrose's new stronghold had gone unnoticed, he was mistaken.

Hardly had the cowboy returned over the skyline of Manzanita Hill than an excited Mexican cook dashed out of the Triangle S kitchen, yelling and waving his arms as he sprinted toward Melrose and Everett Kingman.

The cook was Juan Fernandez, who until recently had been a member of Señor Giboso's smuggling ring. But Melrose, having taken over the control of the Mexitex Land & Cattle Syndicate, had forsaken the dangerous game of contraband shipments over the border, to give his full energies to the profitable career of running Yaqui County's cattle range.

Most of Melrose's cattlemen were ex-members of the smuggling outfit he had ramrodded in the disguise of Señor Giboso. And the job of ranch

248

cook had gone to Juan Fernandez, the peon who had been forced to turn over Hap Kingman and a shipment of narcotics to the border patrol.

"Señor! Señor!" babbled Fernandez, skidding to a halt alongside a corral fence where Everett Kingman and the syndicate boss were inspecting some new breeding stock. "I see a ghost, señor, but eet was not a ghost."

Melrose jerked his cigar from his teeth and said impatiently, "You've been hitting the mescal too heavy, Juan. Get back to peelin' spuds!"

The Mexican shook his head wildly.

"No, no, Señor Melrose! It is Señor Hap King-man—I see him again, weeth my own eyes, *es verdad*! Husking corn I was, in the *cocina*. I saw Hap Kingman ride his *caballo* down Manzanita Hill, *es seguro*—and then he turned and rode away!"

A muscle twitched in Melrose's cheek. Cold dread kindled in his slitted eyes.

"You must be loco, Juan. Hap Kingman is dead—"

Everett Kingman gulped audibly and reminded his chief:

"Don't forget that Hap's carcass wasn't discovered along with his hoss, when the sheriff come back with Joe Ashfield. There's a chance Hap pulled through, chief. An' first thing he'd do would be to come back an' try to look up Anna—"

Melrose turned grimly to Everett Kingman.

"Rustle up some of the boys and ride to Mexitex," he rasped. "If you spot Hap Kingman, gun him down and light a shuck for the Rio. Hide out in Maduro until I send for you—but *don't let Hap Kingman escape alive!*"

24

THUNDERING GUNS

HAP KINGMAN arrived in Mexitex during the siesta hour, so that his return "from the dead" occasioned no excitement, the sun-baked streets being empty.

He dismounted in front of the jailhouse, but found the sheriff's office locked.

Accordingly, the cowboy made his way to the outskirts of town, in the direction of the public cemetery. There, in a little white cottage where Bob Reynolds and his wife had lived ever since the days when Reynolds was a deputy under Les Kingman, the cowboy presented himself at the sheriff's door.

To his surprise, it was opened by Anna Siebert.

"It's me, Anna." Hap grinned as he saw the girl blanch and cling to the door jamb for support. "I'm no ghost—"

He was not prepared for what happened next.

With a sudden burst of tears, Anna Siebert flung herself into his arms, clinging to him as she might her own father. And the cowpuncher, whose busy life on the Kingman Ranch had brought little opportunity for the companionship of women, found his heart stirring with a strange thrill as he rubbed his jaw against the soft clusters of chestnut hair.

"Hap . . . Hap . . . we had given you up . . . long ago . . . for dead," whispered the girl in a hysteria of relief. "And now you've come back . . . you've come back—"

A moment later the sheriff and his gray-haired wife were rushing to the door to greet the supposedly dead cowboy. Bob Reynolds was quick to note the lines which pain had stamped on Hap Kingman's sun-browned face, and knew that those lines could tell a grim story.

While his trio of friends hung on his every word, Hap Kingman haltingly outlined what had happened to him from the morning he and Joe Ashfield had set out from Marfa, bound for the Triangle S spread with the syndicate money from El Paso.

Sheriff Reynolds nodded understandingly as the cowboy outlined his long stay at the badlands home of One-eye Allen, and the probability of their blood relationship.

"All I know is that there are a pair of graves out in boothill, marked Warren and Eleanor Allen," said the sheriff's wife when the cowboy had completed his narrative. "I saw your foster-mother, Florence Kingman, puttin' flowers on them mounds many the time. But I never knew who those graves belonged to."

Kingman turned to Anna Siebert, who had clung to his hand throughout his long discourse.

"Anna," said the cowboy, completely oblivious to the presence of the sheriff and his wife, "I'd have told you I was fond of you before this, I reckon, only I figgered I was an outlaw, the son of an outlaw, Dev Hewett. But now I reckon there's nothin' to stop me. I—"

Kingman broke off in conclusion, aware of the kindly grins of Mr. and Mrs. Reynolds. He leaned back, conscious of the fact that Anna Siebert's eyes glowed with a strange light as they followed every changing expression on his face.

"And what's gone on durin' the past seven weeks here in Mexitex?" he asked his three listeners. "I darn near blundered into a hornet's nest this mornin', over at the Triangle S. Saw Melrose and my brother Everett over there—"

Cold despair quenched the love which had glistened unashamed in Anna Siebert's eyes.

"Melrose moved in with legal possession papers," blurted the sheriff. "Anna's been livin' with us. An' we been powerless to do anything against that lawyer. All the evidence we got against him is circumstantial."

Anna Siebert spoke heavily:

"And Melrose is powerful now. He's crowded

out all the honest men that used to be in dad's syndicate. He controls all the best grazing land, all the waterholes. He's got the whip hand, and he's using it. Honest men don't dare buck him, because Melrose has surrounded himself with killers."

The sheriff stood up, hitching his gun belts.

"Hap, you come over to the county prosecutor's office with me," said the lawman briskly. "We'll lay our cards on the table, an' see if I can't get a warrant to arrest Melrose for the murder of Joe Ashfield. If we can make that charge stick, maybe we can put the cattle syndicate back in Anna's control, where it belongs."

The two men left the house and headed for the courthouse building, restraining a desire to break into a run.

Both realized that events were rapidly shaping themselves toward a climax. Hap Kingman's return would give the county prosecutor and the sheriff some tangible basis for starting proceedings against Russ Melrose, before the latter became unshakeably intrenched as the ramrod of the county's beef range.

"I'll rustle up a good posse and deputize 'em before we go out to force a showdown with Melrose," chuckled the sheriff excitedly. "It'll turn into a damned range war if Melrose once gets wind of what's—*look out!*"

Sheriff Reynolds bawled the warning, even

as they were crossing a side street on their way toward the courthouse.

At the same time the sheriff flung out an arm to pull Hap Kingman to the ground with him.

Brrrrrrang! A hail of bullets whistled overhead, as the two men dropped.

Fifty yards up the street, a close-bunched group of horsemen were triggering six-guns in their direction, their quarry caught in the open.

Horses trumpeted with alarm as their riders sent a third burst of shots at Reynolds and Hap Kingman, as the two began scuttling for the shelter of a nearby lumber yard.

"It's my brother Everett!" panted Hap, as they gained the refuge of the lumber pile. "And he's sided by Melrose's greasers, or I'm a loco leppie!"

The sudden and totally unexpected fusillade had filled the air with gunsmoke above the mounted group of horsemen. Now, seeing that their bullets had failed to find a target, Everett Kingman and his henchmen from the Triangle S spread turned and spurred wildly in the direction of the Rio Grande.

"We'll trail them skunks to hell an' back, Hap!" yelled the sheriff, as the two men emerged from hiding with six-guns drawn. "If they cross into Chihuahua, we'll cross, too, boundary or no boundary!"

Men were running out of saloons and other

buildings as Sheriff Bob Reynolds sprinted down the street, Hap Kingman at his side.

Yelling for men to saddle their horses to form a posse, Reynolds suddenly broke off as he saw Hap Kingman crumple and sprawl headlong, like a man who has stopped a bullet.

Instantly Reynolds was at the cowboy's side, noting that Hap's face was gray with pain as the sheriff assisted him to his feet.

"It's my leg," gritted the cowboy. "Haven't exercised it enough. I'm afraid I won't be able to go with the posse, Bob. But don't wait for me—"

Ten minutes later, Hap Kingman leaned against a saloon wall and muttered disappointed oaths as he saw Sheriff Reynolds head toward the Rio Grande, with a score or more of townspeople riding with him, all armed to the teeth.

Everett Kingman and his would-be ambushers, dashing past the startled border patrol officials, had crossed the Rio Grande and were riding for the security of the Chihuahua hills.

But the sheriff and his hastily organized posse, with an outlaw trail to follow, were disregarding political boundaries to swarm over onto Mexican soil in hot pursuit of Everett Kingman and his Mexican killers from the Triangle S.

Hap Kingman, sick with disappointment and half nauseated by the pain of wrenched tendons in his leg, hobbled his way painfully to the coroner's office across the street.

There he greeted the deputy coroner, Dan Kendelhardt, who was among the few witnesses of the attempted murder of the two men by Everett Kingman and his horsemen.

"Gripes me to think I can't be in on the shoot-out," said Hap Kingman, as he saw the sheriff's posse disappear into the cactus-dotted Mexican hills beyond the river. "Reynolds has got that dry-gulchin' gang outnumbered, and I don't reckon he'll come back until he's draggin' those owlhooters with him."

The deputy coroner nodded glumly.

"If those skunks are workin' for Russ Melrose, I hope they get caught," agreed Kendelhardt. "Me an' the sheriff have been doin' some thinkin' about Doc Hanson's disappearance, an' I wouldn't be surprised if Russ Melrose don't know the answer to that one, too."

Through the doorway of the coroner's office, Hap Kingman scanned the Purple Hawk Saloon, across the street.

Painted on the office windows of the upper story was a sign that twisted Kingman's lips in a bitter grin:

RUSSELL MELROSE
Attorney-at-law

"There's no need of me stickin' around doin' nothin' while the sheriff is out chasin' those skunks who tried to kill me just now," said Hap Kingman. "I think there's a little business I can attend to very handily, myself!"

While the deputy coroner looked on wonderingly, the cowboy limped his way across the street and headed up the stairs leading to Russ Melrose's business office.

25

INSIDE MELROSE'S SAFE

HAP KINGMAN had a definite reason for what he was about to do. Hap figured that inside Melrose's office he might be able to recover the contents of the money belt which the crooked lawyer had stolen from Joe Ashfield's body.

It was a fifty-fifty chance, but a lot would hinge on the recovery of that money. He knew that Melrose would not dare to deposit the stolen funds in the Mexitex bank. And, since the lawyer still maintained his business offices, it was probable that his safe might contain the missing cash.

He entered Melrose's office without the formality of a knock, and grinned as he recognized the scrawny figure of Barney Adams, the law clerk who handled Melrose's routine office business for as long as Kingman could remember.

The rawboned clerk had just turned from the window as Kingman entered, his face bleak.

"I reckon you saw what happened out on the street just now," Kingman rasped, his eyes darting to the huge black safe in one corner of the room.

Adams gulped, and his hands shook nervously as he adjusted the green eyeshade perched over his furrowed brow.

"I . . . I heard shooting," confessed Melrose's assistant. "But what . . . what do you want?"

Kingman grinned crookedly. He paused in midroom, thumb hooked in cartridge belt.

"That shooting was done under orders of your boss, Russ Melrose," snapped the cowboy. "And I'm here on business that concerns Melrose. Adams, I'm orderin' you to unlock that safe of Melrose's, and do it pronto, without arguin' with me."

Adams sagged into a swivel chair, his face draining to the dirty yellow color of banana meat.

"I . . . I can't open that safe without orders from Melrose," Adams protested weakly. "I . . . I don't know the combination—"

Kingman slid his Colt .45 from holster.

"Maybe a dose of lead poisonin' would refresh yore memory, Barney. I got plumb urgent business regardin' the contents of that safe."

Barney Adams stared at the black bore of Kingman's .45 and shook his head in panic.

"It ain't legal . . . it's robbery!" squawked the law clerk. "I can't do it!"

The sound of Kingman's Colt coming to full cock made the law clerk forget the technicalities of the moment. Adams scuttled crablike to the safe, spun the polished combination dial, and then yanked the black handle to operate the tumblers.

As the door of the vault opened, Hap Kingman stepped forward swiftly in time to see Barney Adams reach into the opened safe and turn with a black-muzzled six-gun in his own palsied hand. With a swift outward blow of his own gun barrel, Kingman dropped Melrose's office assistant before Adams could trigger a bullet in his direction.

Rolling the unconscious clerk to one side, Hap Kingman holstered his gun and squatted down to begin pulling out steel drawers from the safe.

He riffled swiftly through filed legal papers. One compartment yielded a canvas sack bearing the name of the local bank. It contained upward of a hundred dollars in loose change and packages of dollar bills.

He had gone through the contents of Melrose's safe for the third time before he was forced to admit failure. There was no sign of Joe Ashfield's money belt inside the vault, nor money which could conceivably be traced to the loot which Melrose had taken from the Triangle S foreman's corpse out in the Sierra Secos almost two months past.

"He must have it cached somewhere over at Siebert's ranchhouse, then," decided Kingman, his voice tinged with disappointment. "I reckon

I bashed Adams on the noggin for no good purpose, after all."

A heavy brown envelope was in a compartment marked "Personal," and it contained an object which Kingman had not yet examined—an object too light in bulk to be Ashfield's money belt.

Nevertheless, the cowboy opened the envelope. Into his waiting palm dropped a small silver snuffbox, the metal tarnished with age.

Curiously, Hap Kingman opened the lid of the snuffbox, and then squatted there motionless, eyes staring at the tintype photograph which was glued on the inner side of the lid.

It was almost an exact duplicate of the tintype which One-eye Allen had showed him—a picture of Warren and Eleanor Allen with their baby son. Costumes and background were identical to the picture which One-eye Allen had said was taken nineteen years before by a San Antonio photographer.

With fingers which suddenly shook, Hap Kingman lifted the contents of the snuffbox into the light. It was a tightly folded bit of soft sheepskin, and covering one side of the leather was some sort of map, traced onto the sheepskin with a hot needle that had left fine lines like a pen dipped in brownish-black ink.

"My father's gold-mine map—"

A shiver coursed down Hap Kingman's spine as he realized the significance of what he had found in Russ Melrose's safe. This, beyond a shadow of a doubt, was the map to the lost gold claim which One-eye Allen had said was the possession of his missing brother, Warren.

How could it have come into Russ Melrose's hands ?

There was but one answer to that, and that realization left Hap Kingman limp.

"Melrose was the red-masked killer who shot my father and mother—the hombre I been wantin' to get revenge on all these years!"

Parts of the weird jigsaw puzzle fell into place now.

Melrose had told him that he was the son of Dev Hewett, a long-dead outlaw. That outlaw had left in trust with Melrose a notched six-gun as his only legacy—that, and a dying request that his son kill George Siebert to avenge his death.

"I can see it all now," whispered Hap Kingman, clamping his father's sheepskin treasure map in a damp fist. "Melrose knew that Everett was really Hewett's son, and that I was Warren Allen's son. Les Kingman adopted the two of us—and when we came of age, and I told Melrose I was honin' to avenge my father's death—"

It was crystal clear, now, in the light of this evidence which had lain through the years in Melrose's private safe.

Melrose, seeking to obtain control of the cattle syndicate headed by George Siebert, had deliberately led Hap to believe that George Siebert was the rightful target for all the festering hate that had burned in the cowboy's heart as a result of his terrible babyhood memories—

A slight noise behind him snapped Hap Kingman back to earth. He turned his head, expecting to see that the law clerk, Barney Adams, had returned to his senses.

Then Kingman froze as he saw a sombrero-clad man standing in the doorway, almost out of the range of his vision.

"Hold it, Kingman!"

It was the voice of Russ Melrose that snarled the low-voiced order, as Kingman reached instinctively for his gun butt.

The leering Mexitex lawyer came into the room and closed the door. A cocked .45 six-gun was in his fist, its black bore leveled unwaveringly at Kingman's body.

"Doing a little private investigating among my private papers?" leered Melrose, halting a few steps away. "Well, get your arms up. One booger move, and I blast you to hell!"

Hap Kingman dropped the tarnished sterling snuffbox and the sweat-moist sheepskin map. He elevated his hands to the level of his shoulders and then stood slowly erect.

"You're going to shoot me down like a rat, Melrose," said the cowboy, his voice registering bleakly. "But before you shoot—answer me this:

Dev Hewett is Everett's real father, isn't he? *My real name is Allen?*"

Melrose's eyes slitted warily. Then he nodded gravely.

"It won't hurt for you to know it now. Yeah—I switched yore identities. I figgered to use you to wipe out George Siebert, so I could move in on his syndicate. I admit things didn't run so smooth—but they led to the right end. I'm sittin' pretty in Yaqui County—and you've drawed a one-way ticket to hell."

There was a moment's silence, broken only by Barney Adam's moans. Melrose moved closer, the knuckle of his trigger finger turning white under slowly increasing pressure.

"If you got any prayers to say, hop to it, Kingman!" whispered Melrose. "I'm killing you, and making it look as if you and Adams there had a shootout while you were robbing my safe. My own hide isn't secure as long as you're above ground, Kingman."

Hap's muscles stiffened before the anticipated shock of the bullet that would blast him into eternity with a whit more pressure of Melrose's trigger finger!

Thoughts shot like lightning through Hap Kingman's brain during the clipped second of time that he waited for the six-gun to roar and flash in Melrose's grip.

Then an inspiration came, and the cowboy

seized it as a drowning man clutches at the proverbial straw:

"You're throwin' away a gold mine if you pull that trigger, Melrose."

The lawyer's hand relaxed.

"Meaning what, cowboy? If you think you can talk your way out of this, you got another think comin'."

Kingman moved his boot toe to direct the taut-nerved lawyer's attention to the unfolded gold-mine map on the floor at his feet.

"You've kept that silver snuffbox in your safe for eighteen years, Melrose. Isn't that right?"

The lawyer's nostrils dilated nervously. Alert for treachery, still Melrose was intrigued by the doomed cowboy's words.

"Maybe so. What you drivin' at?"

New hope leaped in Kingman's heart, as a faint chance of outwitting Russ Melrose was born in his head.

"That box contained a map showin' where my real father had a gold mine. Mebbe you didn't know that, Melrose."

The lawyer rubbed his jaw thoughtfully.

"How come you know so much about that sheepskin map, Kingman?"

"What did you think I was ransackin' your safe for just now?"

Melrose looked puzzled.

"I figured maybe you were hunting that money

belt I took off Joe Ashfield's corpse. In which case you were drilling a dry well, Hap—because that dinero is salted away in my safe out at the Triangle S ranchhouse, where I can keep an eye on it."

The lawyer moved closer, jabbing his six-gun muzzle into the cowboy's stomach while he reached out and drew forth the six-gun from Kingman's holster.

"Now," said the lawyer, backing away, "tell me what you know about that map, Kingman."

Thinking fast, the cowboy decided to confide part of the truth to Melrose.

It would be a grim battle of wits, with his own life at stake, and he could not afford to play the wrong card.

"You may be curious to know why I didn't feed the buzzards after you left me pinned down under a dead horse," Hap began. "That—"

Melrose snarled out an impatient oath.

"Get to the point, Kingman. Stick to the subject of that gold map, and what you know about it."

Kingman's eyes slitted. The cards were beginning to fall his way, now.

"That's what I'm drivin' at. Melrose, I was found out there in the Sierra Secos by the man who was with my father when that map was drawn. One-eye Allen, who happens to be my uncle. It was One-eye Allen who set my broken leg and nursed me back to health."

Greed made Melrose's narrow-set eyes glitter. "Go on."

"Well, to make it brief—One-eye Allen knows where that mine is, or can locate it with the aid of this map. If you hadn't surprised me lootin' your safe just now, I would have taken this map to One-eye Allen—and the map would have made him rich."

Russ Melrose's breath came in short jerky gusts. A pulse hammered on the knotted blue veins across his forehead.

"Where's One-eye Allen at?" he demanded craftily.

Kingman laughed shortly.

"You'd like to know, wouldn't you, Melrose? Well, I'll make a bargain with you. I'll take you to One-eye Allen, and you can dicker with him about that map. He'll make you a half partner in the gold mine—a mine you couldn't locate without Allen's help, and a mine which Allen couldn't locate without the aid of that map."

"And what's your price—what's your side of the bargain?"

Kingman grinned at the avarice in the lawyer's tone. But he knew that, for the time being at least, he was safe from the threat of the lawyer's gun.

"I'll take you to One-eye Allen on the promise that you spare my life. That you'll let me get out of Texas for keeps."

Melrose hid the triumph which leaped within

him. Ever since the night he had murdered Warren Allen and his wife, to obtain the gold map which he had kept ever since in his safe, Russ Melrose had fumed at the dirty deal fate had handed him.

The sheepskin map represented untold riches, and yet the map was useless unless he knew what part of the frontier the man's directions applied to.

Now, through a bewildering series of circumstances, fate had dealt him a royal flush. The map he had kept through the years might yet prove to be a key to unlock a fabulous golden fortune out of the badlands which had held the secret thus far.

"O.K., Hap!" grated the lawyer. "I give you my word to turn you loose, as soon as you take me to this one-eyed uncle of yours. I know you're speakin' truth, otherwise you wouldn't know what this map was that I shot your father and mother to get."

Kingman went white at this cold-blooded confession which confirmed his own hunch as to Melrose's guilt. The knowledge that Russ Melrose had been the red-masked man of mystery, who for so many years had haunted Hap's adolescent dreams, now left the cowboy with a sickish feeling in the pit of his stomach.

He knew that Russ Melrose intended to double-cross him; the lawyer's guile was transparent. But Kingman knew also that he possessed an ace in the hole—that if he maneuvered things right, he could lead Melrose into a trap from which there would be no possible escape.

"Where is One-eye Allen now?" demanded Melrose.

"Out in the Sierra Secos."

"*Bueno*. We start tonight. In the meantime, Kingman, I got to tie you up, gag you, and put you in safekeeping. The sheriff is liable to wonder where you are, and as you might have been seen coming into my office here, I got to make sure nobody'll find you if they get to searching."

26

BACK FROM MEXICO

THE varied hues of sunset were reflected on the ripples of the Rio Grande when Sheriff Bob Reynolds and a trail-dusty posse of Mexitex citizens rode back across the international bridge.

Their man hunt into the Chihuahua malpais had not been unsuccessful, as testified by the three handcuffed Mexican killers who were being brought back surrounded by deputies.

Proof that their victory had been obtained only at heavy cost was evident in the four dead possemen who were strapped to their saddles, corpses riddled by outlaw lead.

"Caught up with 'em, eh, Sheriff?" asked a border-patrol officer, unlocking the big border gate to admit the returning posse to American soil.

The lawman nodded glumly. The Federal man noticed that Reynolds' head was swathed in bloody bandages.

"Cornered 'em in a box canyon over toward Las Piedras Pass. These greasers surrendered rather than shoot it out."

The border-patrol inspector searched the faces of the Mexican prisoners.

"Didn't get Everett Kingman?"

The sheriff shook his head glumly.

"Everett vamoosed on us. But he dasn't show his face around Yaqui County any more—not after tryin' to shoot me an' Hap Kingman in broad daylight."

Reynolds took his prisoners to the jailhouse and turned them over to the custody of his turnkey.

The stiffening bodies of his slain possemen Reynolds removed to Doc Hanson's morgue in the rear of the undertaking parlors.

Dan Kendelhardt, the assistant coroner who was handling Hanson's business ever since the old sawbones had mysteriously disappeared during Hap Kingman's murder trail months before, took the sheriff aside after the glum-faced possemen had departed.

"Sheriff, I'm worried about Hap Kingman."

"What about him?"

"He went over to Melrose's law office just after you fellers rode across the border this afternoon. I ain't seen him since. I saw Russ Melrose go into his office shortly afterward, but Melrose came out alone."

The sheriff's face betrayed his alarm.

"Looks bad. Hear any shots?"

"No," replied Kendelhardt. "You figger those two might shoot it out?"

The sheriff removed his six-gun from holster, twirled the cylinder and replaced it.

"Hard tellin'. I'll go over to Melrose's office for a look-see. If you saw Hap go in, an' he didn't come out, then he must still be there."

The sheriff climbed the stairs to the upper floor of the Purple Hawk Saloon, and drew his Colt .45 as he approached Melrose's office. A light burned inside, and the pasty-faced law clerk, Barney Adams, opened the door upon the sheriff's knock.

"Where's Hap Kingman?"

The clerk started violently as Reynolds shoved his way into Melrose's office.

"I don't know," Adams said.

"Didn't he come here?"

Adams pointed to a blue welt the size of a hen's egg which had disfigured his bald scalp.

"He sure did, Sheriff. I was aiming to report it to you. Kingman came in this afternoon, either drunk or mad. He conked me with a gun butt—and when I came to, he was gone."

The sheriff looked startled.

"Can't figure why Hap should want to conk you. Where's Russ Melrose?"

Adams shrugged.

"Melrose brought me to. Then he left. That window was open, so Melrose figured Kingman crawled out on the porch roof, jumped across to that gambling-hall roof, and got out that way.

Leastwise, Melrose didn't meet Kingman comin' out."

The sheriff scowled with worry.

Barney Adams' story had a distinctly false note to it, regarding Hap Kingman's strange behavior. Still, his explanation of the cowboy's method of exit would explain why Dan Kendelhardt had not seen Kingman leave the lawyer's offices.

"Somethin' damned fishy here, Adams. If you're lyin', I'll choke the truth out of you. Meanwhile, I'll poke around a little."

The sheriff's search of Melrose's office was brief but thorough. There was no place that could hide a corpse, in the event that Kingman had been murdered here.

A thorough search of a clothes closet and adjoining office where Adams' files were cabineted revealed no clues as to Kingman's disappearance.

Grave-faced with worry, Sheriff Reynolds left the Purple Hawk Saloon and hurried to his own home. Neither his wife nor Anna Siebert had seen any trace of the cowboy since he had departed in company with the sheriff earlier that afternoon.

"This business o' people disappearin' in broad daylight is gettin' on my nerves," groaned the sheriff. "Why should Hap visit Melrose's office? An' why should he knock out Barney Adams? It don't make sense."

At that moment, Hap Kingman was alive, but

extremely uncomfortable. He was bound hand and foot with braided rawhide rope, and gagged with a bandanna knotted on his neck nape. The liquor-storage cellar of the Purple Hawk Saloon was his temporary prison.

The cowboy, kept in check by a gun hidden in Russ Melrose's coat pocket, had been marched down into the saloon barroom by a back stairway.

There, money had changed hands between Melrose and the Purple Hawk bartender, and Hap Kingman had been ushered down into the wine cellar where he had been tied up and left in total darkness.

The cowboy had no way of keeping track of time, in the blackness of the saloon cellar; but he knew that it was nearing midnight when the door was unlocked and Russ Melrose appeared.

"I got horses in the alley behind the saloon," said the lawyer. "I'm leaving your wrists tied together, Kingman. We're heading for the Sierra Secos while it's dark."

Melrose untied the cowboy, allowed him to stretch his stiffened muscles, and then prodded him up the stairs with a gun muzzle.

He was ushered down a corridor and out a back door opening on a narrow alley behind the saloon—an alley where, on another grim night, Melrose had carried away the knife-slashed corpse of Dr. Harry Hanson on his way to a watery grave on the bottom of the Rio Grande—a grave from which the ill-fated medico had never returned.

A pair of saddled horses whickered at the men as they walked down the alley in the darkness.

They mounted silently, and rode out into a deserted side street which intersected the main stem.

Saddlebags had been packed with provisions for a several-day trek into the Sierra Secos badlands, Kingman noticed, and tarpaulin-wrapped soogan rolls had been strapped behind each saddle cantle.

Not until they were a mile away from Mexitex headed in the general direction of the Sierra Secos mountains, did Russ Melrose remove the six-gun from his pocket and holster it.

A crescent moon lifted above the saw-toothed eastern horizon, and by its phantom glow Hap Kingman saw the grim face of his captor, eyes regarding him with blinkless fixity.

"From now on, you're the guide," grunted Russ Melrose. "Where abouts is this One-eye Allen camped?"

Kingman, his wrists still bound with rawhide, pointed vaguely toward the wastelands ahead of them.

"Yonderward. I'm not tellin' you where."

Melrose's lips twitched with suppressed anger.

"If you're double-crossin' me, Kingman—"

The cowboy laughed hollowly. "My life's at

stake, Melrose. My stayin' alive depends on livin' up to my bargain to lead you to One-eye Allen."

They pushed on in silence, Kingman taking the trail which led toward the foothills.

Triumph was welling in Melrose's heart. Safe in an inner pocket of his coat was the sheepskin map which he had murdered Warren Allen to obtain, almost two decades before.

Once Melrose had located the gold vein which that map represented, he would pay off with hot lead, and not with freedom for the cowboy.

The sickle-shaped moon climbed in the starry heavens as they reached the base of the foothills and headed on into the desolate, cactus-dotted desert country.

The trail was narrow and rocky, and Hap Kingman rode in the lead. If he was worried, he did not show it. He lifted his voice in a plaintive cowboy melody, ceasing only on a curt order from his captor.

A night owl hooted in the sky overhead. Somewhere, miles away, a lone coyote bayed at the moon, his solitary howls sounded magnified by echo, like an entire pack of the predatory beasts.

The clip-clop of steel-shod hoofs made faint echoes against the rim-rocks of dry washes as they rode past. Both men rode in silence, each wrapped in his own thoughts.

Then, from out of a clump of chaparral which flanked the trail on their left, came a high-pitched voice like an off-key clarinet with a squeaky reed:

"Reach for a cloud, you buskies! The first man who reaches for a hogleg is a dead man!"

Hap Kingman reined up and lifted his tied-together hands, but a grin was on his face.

Russ Melrose made a darting motion toward his gun, then thought better of it as a bowlegged hombre stepped out of ambush and leveled a Winchester at his midriff.

"Good work, unk!" Kingman said to One-eye Allen. "I was dependin' on you to spring my man trap!"

27

JAIL FOR A MALO HOMBRE

MELROSE made a gagging sound as One-eye Allen stepped forward, his single eye squinting at the mounted lawyer down the sights of his .30-30.

"You damned, double-crossing skunk!" bellowed Melrose, lifting his arms shakily. "You—"

Hap Kingman swung out of stirrups and stood grinning at the lawyer.

"What you mean by those insultin' words, Mr. Melrose?" asked the cowboy mockingly. "My part of the bargain was to lead you to One-eye Allen. I'm keepin' that bargain, here and now. And—whether you want to or not—you're keepin' your part of the deal. I'm not your prisoner now—I'm as free as a sneeze."

One-eye Allen reached up and removed Melrose's gun from holster. Then, aiming his rifle at the lawyer's head, he ordered Melrose to dismount.

"Untie that rope that Hap's wearin'," ordered the bony prospector. "We'll use the same piggin' string to tie your mitts together, I reckon."

Not until Hap Kingman had completed the happy task of knotting his own bounds on Melrose's hairy wrists did the old hardrock miner relax.

"Lord, son, but I was worried when you didn't show up on schedule," Allen said. "I was fixin' to leave for Mexitex town, come daylight, to see what was goin' on down there."

Hap Kingman reached under Melrose's lapel and drew forth a flat silver snuffbox.

Then, taking the lawyer's six-gun from his uncle, Hap passed over the box and the sheepskin map which it contained.

"There's your gold claim, unk—a bit late, but just as good as the day my father drawed it!" Hap Kingman chuckled. "And I sort of got a hunch that my dad's ghost is around somewhere, laughin' right this minute. Melrose took good care of that map all these years."

Sweat beaded Melrose's face and twinkled in the moonlight as the lawyer saw One-eye Allen unfold the pliable sheepskin and squint at the familiar markings on the leather.

"That gold claim's as good as found ag'in, Hap!" cried the prospector, as he saw an end to his long search. "I know the general location this map describes, and Warren's put down all the important landmarks I'll need to know."

Hap Kingman, holding a careless drop on the helpless lawyer, turned to his excited uncle.

"You roll up your soogans and traipse back into the Sierra Secos tomorrow, unk," said the cowboy. "Soon as you got the claim located, you light a shuck down to Mexitex and record it. And maybe, if you're not too long doin' it, you'll have the pleasure of seeing Russ Melrose stretch hang rope, to boot."

The old prospector thrust the long-lost map into a pocket of his Levi's, and paused a moment to regard the tintype photograph of his brother in the lid of the snuffbox.

"You sure you can get this jigger back to town?" he asked anxiously.

"Why not?" Hap grinned. "He'll be roostin' in the calaboose before sunrise."

The old prospector thrust out a scrawny hand.

"Half o' that gold claim is yours, son. It's rightfully yours, as a sort o' legacy from your father."

Hap Kingman, remembering that a notched six-gun had been the only legacy he had had to look forward to a short time before, gave his uncle's hand an extra shake.

"Forget it, unk. Cows're my business, not grubbin' gold out of quartz ledges."

He turned to Melrose and motioned toward the lawyer's horse.

"Straddle that bronc, hombre," commanded the puncher. "I'm plumb anxious to get you back to town and turn you over to Bob Reynolds. He'll have a cell all dusted out for you in his *juzgado*.

You'll have plenty of time to think of who you want for a lawyer, before your case comes to trial."

A few minutes later, when he had remounted his own bronc, Hap Kingman leaned down to bid his new-found uncle good-bye.

"Sounds pretty flat to say I'm glad I met up with a relative I didn't know I had, unk." The cowboy chuckled. "And by the time you drift back to Mexitex, maybe I'll have a new niece-in-law to introduce to you."

One-eye Allen waved in farewell as Kingman moved with his sullen prisoner.

"*Hasta la vista*, Hap. An' congratulate yore Anna for me."

Mexitex town was shaken out of its lethargy the next day when news traveled from bar to bar throughout the border settlement regarding the startling events of the previous night.

From the sheriff's office had come announcements that the erstwhile county judge and cow-country lawyer, Russ Melrose, was lodged in Bob Reynolds' jailhouse *incommunicado*, charged with murder, smuggling, and sundry lesser crimes.

The news was received with consternation among the cowhands at Melrose's Triangle S ranch, and for reasons of their own, the ranch crew saddled up and disappeared in the general direction of the Mexican border.

At any rate, when Hap Kingman accompanied

the sheriff out to Siebert's ranch the day following his arrival in Mexitex with his prisoner,
they found the place deserted. There was evidence in the bunkhouse to indicate that Melrose's
henchmen had packed their warbags in haste,
not even troubling to water or feed the stock
remaining in the ranch corrals.

A diligent search of the ranchouse by Kingman
and the old lawman brought to light a small
iron safe which Russ Melrose had hidden in a
bedroom closet.

The safe responded to a charge of dynamite,
and among the contents was a money belt which
Kingman identified as being the one which Joe
Ashfield, the ill-fated Triangle S *segundo*, had
been wearing at the time of his return from El
Paso.

Still intact inside the money belt was nearly
thirty thousand dollars in greenbacks, belonging
to the Mexitex Land & Cattle Syndicate.

Likewise in the safe was the deed to Anna
Siebert's Triangle S spread, and the unpaid mortgage paper bearing George Siebert's signature.

"Fixin' all this up will be a matter for the
courts," said Sheriff Reynolds, "but from where
I sit it looks like Anna Siebert is boss o' her
father's cattle syndicate again."

The sheriff gave Hap Kingman a sidelong
glance.

"Anna'll be needin' another foreman. Runnin'

a syndicate is a man's job, anyway," he said pointedly. "Offhand, Hap, I'd say you had as good a chance as any to land that job. Or would you object to workin' for a lady boss?"

Hap Kingman colored under the sheriff's gibe.

"What wife *ain't* a man's boss?" he countered. "Let's get goin', Sheriff. I want to be the first to tell Anna the good news. I mean, about locatin' Ashfield's stolen dinero again, damn you!"

The ruddy glow of the setting sun was in their eyes as they rode down to Mexitex and headed for the sheriff's home on the outer reaches of the cow town.

They dismounted in front of the house and announced their arrival with boisterous whoops, intended to bring Mrs. Reynolds and Anna Siebert to the door.

Instead, silence greeted them as Sheriff Reynolds opened the door and stepped into the living room.

An instant later the grizzled old lawman gasped aloud and seized Kingman's arm.

The two men were staring at the sprawled form of Mrs. Reynolds lying prostrate on the rug.

For an instant they thought the woman was dead, and then they saw that she had been clubbed viciously over the left eye, a blow that had split the flesh to the scalp and drenched the old lady's face with crimson.

"Anna!" yelled Hap Kingman, as he saw the sheriff rush to the side of his unconscious mate. "Anna!"

The name was flung back in empty echo from the walls of the room.

"Get me some water in the kitchen, Hap!" said the sheriff, his voice breaking with grief.

The cowboy, his face blanched with dread, headed for the kitchen door. As he passed the living room table, his attention was arrested by a hastily scrawled letter which lay displayed on the dark wood.

Snatching up the paper, Hap Kingman read:

SHERIFF: I'm holding Anna Siebert hostage until midnight. If Russ Melrose ain't out of jail and safe in Mexico then, the girl will feed the catfish in the Rio Grande.

EVERETT KINGMAN.

An overwhelming sense of loss dazed Hap Kingman as he mechanically made his way to the kitchen and returned with a pitcher of water.

He sank dazedly into a chair, staring at his foster brother's brief kidnap note, while the frantic sheriff bathed his wife's face with cold water.

"Everett did this, Sheriff!" Kingman said finally, as Mrs. Reynolds' eyelids fluttered and her face began to be restored to its natural color. "He's kidnapped Anna."

The sheriff did not appear to hear. He tenderly lifted his wife's limp form and carried her to a nearby divan.

It was ten minutes before the lawman's wife had recovered sufficiently to give an account of what had happened. The news seemed to stun Sheriff Bob Reynolds, but Hap had already guessed most of the details:

"Anna and I were piecing a quilt out in the dining room. We heard hoofbeats outside, and someone knocking hard on the door. I . . . I went to answer it, and Everett Kingman came in."

The woman buried her face in her hands, shuddering at the memory she was trying to recapture inside her addled brain.

"He was murderous. Wild-eyed. Said he'd got back from Mexico . . . last night . . . and heard about Melrose being . . . jailed."

The sheriff and Kingman exchanged glances.

They knew that Everett Kingman had come to Reynolds' home to shoot it out with the sheriff. Everett was probably half drunk at the time, and mescal always gave him false courage. Otherwise, Hap knew that his foster-brother would never have dared ride north of the border.

"I . . . I told him that you weren't here . . . that you were out of town. He said he had come to kill you, Bob!" The quivering old lady gripped

286

her husband's hand in a shuddering grasp. "I told Everett you were out of town on business. And then . . . Anna came in . . . she headed for the rifle hanging above the fireplace . . . to drive Everett away."

Mrs. Reynolds groped a palsied hand to the bruise on her head.

"I remember Everett striking me with his pistol," whispered the old lady. "I remember Anna screaming. Then . . . all seemed to . . . fade away . . . into a black emptiness."

Hap Kingman crossed the room and handed the sheriff the hastily scrawled kidnap demand which Everett had left behind.

"Everett was smart enough to know that we'd turn Melrose loose in order to get Anna back alive," the cowboy said. "He probably tied her up and put her on his horse and they rode double out of town. Anyway out here on the border to Mexitex there wasn't anybody to see him kidnappin' her."

The sheriff's face hardened as he scanned the note.

"He gives no proof that Anna is even alive," he rasped. "Even if we turned Melrose out of jail, we'd have no way of knowing Anna would get back to us safe."

Something in the sheriff's clipped tone put a cold shock through Kingman.

"We've got to turn Melrose loose. We got to

give Anna the chance Everett says he'll give her."

The sheriff, kneeling beside his wife, locked glances with a white-faced cowboy standing above him.

"Everett's not the one to keep a promise, drunk or sober," replied Reynolds. "If we turned Russ Melrose free now, it would be violatin' my oath of office. I'd feel like I was turnin' a hydrophoby wolf loose to prey on people, Hap. No—it can't be done."

The sheriff's face softened as he saw the bitterness stamped across the cowboy's countenance.

"You know I love Anna—almost as much as a daughter," whispered the veteran lawman. "But I got my duty to do, Hap. When you've got your wits back, you'll see that it would be impossible to turn Russ Melrose loose."

Hap Kingman turned on his heel and strode from the room. Walking out through the blue twilight, the cowboy studied the hoof-trampled soil at the hitch rack.

But there would be no chance of finding Everett Kingman's tracks and following them, even if night were not approaching.

Grimly, Hap Kingman mounted his own horse and spurred into a gallop. He drew rein in a flurry of dust in front of the Mexitex jail.

Inside the lamplighted office was Grandpa Neeley, the jailer. The oldster looked up and grinned as Kingman entered the room, his eyes darting toward the steel-barred door of the cell block.

"What's on yore mind, Hap?" greeted Neeley, swinging about in his swivel chair.

"I've come to take Russ Melrose out of jail."

Neeley's boots hit the floor with a thump.

"You mean Reynolds is transferrin' that varmint to another jail? You mean the customs hombres are makin' a Federal case out o' this, an' cheatin' us o' the pleasure o' hangin' that snake?"

"Yes. *Andale*, Neeley. Hurry up."

The jailer picked up his ring of keys and unlocked the cell-block door. Then he turned, squinting at the cowboy over brass-rimmed spectacles.

"Sheriff give you orders to turn Melrose over to you?"

"I just come from Reynolds' place," evaded the cowboy. "I'm a deputy sheriff. What the hell more authority do you need? You don't figger I'm aimin' to lynch Melrose, do you?"

Neeley shrugged.

"No—not that I'd give a damn what happened to that shyster."

A moment later Russ Melrose appeared in the doorway, frowning in bewilderment. The lawyer had lost weight during his term of imprisonment, and fear was plainly stamped on his visage.

"Come with me, Melrose!" ordered Kingman,

covering the lawyer with a Colt .45. "Neeley, you stick to your knittin'."

Once out on the street, the cowboy stood facing the puzzled lawyer, who was staring wildly about as if expecting to be greeted by a lynch mob.

"What's the idea, Kingman?" demanded the lawyer quaveringly.

"My brother Everett kidnapped Anna Siebert this afternoon," announced the cowboy bluntly. "He's holdin' her hostage for yore safety."

Fresh hope leaped inside Melrose at this totally unexpected news.

"I got a strong hunch," said the cowboy, "that Everett lit a shuck either for the Flyin' K ranch or for that cave on the south bank of the Rio, where your Señor Giboso gang holed up. Leastwise his kidnap note hints he might feed her to the fishes. You and I are ridin' out there, and if Anna hasn't been hurt, I'll swap you for her."

Kingman eyed the row of ponies hitched to the jail's tie rail, and selected a leggy buckskin belonging to one of Reynolds' deputies.

"Fork that buckskin," he told the excited lawyer. "And don't forget that I've got the drop on you. It so happens that this six-gun is the one that belonged to Dev Hewett—and I think it wouldn't be any more than justice comin' to pass if you forced me to make you the fourteenth notch on this hog-leg!"

But Russ Melrose, faced with a chance at

290

freedom which he had not deemed possible five minutes before, was in a cooperative mood. He climbed aboard the deputy's saddle horse, and a few minutes later the two were riding out of town stirrup by stirrup.

Kingman cast apprehensive eyes in the direction of the sheriff's house, as they left the outskirts of the town behind them. But Reynolds had not appeared. Doubtlessly the sheriff was remaining by his injured wife, little dreaming that the cowboy would have the audacity to release Melrose from jail without his official approval.

Night had fallen and the terrain was bathed in the ghostly light of the half moon by the time Kingman and Melrose had reached the Flying K ranch.

At Hap's loud halloo, the ancient Chinese cook, Wing Sing, appeared on the porch of the house where Hap Kingman had been raised to manhood.

"Everett at home?" called the cowboy, his heart pounding anxiously as he waited the Oriental's reply.

"No see Everett long time now," came the cook's answer. "Me hear that no-clount go to Mexico velly fast!"

Kingman refused to be discouraged by Wing Sing's report. He had not expected to find his foster-brother hiding out at their own ranch.

"Everett's probably got spies tipped off in

Mexitex to find out whether you got out of jail," commented the puncher, as he and Melrose headed for the Rio Grande. "But as long as I'm holdin' *your* life forfeit, Melrose, mebbe he won't kill Anna Siebert."

The lawyer swore feverently.

"I'm hoping as much as you are that Everett rattled his hocks over to that cave," said Melrose. "But if he hasn't, what you aiming to do?"

Cold fury throbbed through the cowboy's veins.

"I'm liable to get to rememberin' that it was you who shot my father and mother in cold blood, Melrose," answered Hap. "It'd do me good to put a bullet through your guts and leave you kickin'."

They gained a bottomland trail which flanked the American side of the Rio Grande, and followed it until a bend in the river brought the towering Chihuahua bluff in view, at the base of which Señor Giboso had had his rendezvous.

Kingman drew rein alongside a dead cottonwood.

"I'm tyin' you up here, Melrose," decided the cowboy. "I'll go the rest of the way afoot. If I don't find Everett and the girl, I'll be back pronto. Be sure you keep yore trap close-hobbled."

The lawyer made no protest as Hap Kingman uncoiled his lariat and bound Melrose securely to the bole of the cottonwood.

Then, after picketing their two horses a short distance away, Hap Kingman inspected his six-guns briefly and headed off up the river.

The Rio Grande sluiced over a gravel bar midway between the point where Kingman had halted and the outlaw cavern. The cowboy tugged off boots and chaps, rolled up his Levi's, and waded to the Mexican bank.

Then, replacing his footgear, the cowboy vanished into the thick brush, working his way cautiously toward Señor Giboso's cavern, on the alert for possible Mexican guards.

A few moments after Kingman's departure, Russ Melrose caught the sound of hoofs approaching up the river from the direction of Mexitex.

The rider came into view, and Melrose shrank against the cottonwood trunk as he stared at the oncoming horsemen, fearful lest it be Sheriff Bob Reynolds, riding in pursuit of his errant deputy.

Then, as the rider came abreast of the cotton-wood tree, Melrose lifted his voice in a low shout of triumph.

"Juan! Juan Fernandez!" called the tied-up outlaw, as he recognized his Mexican henchman. "Come over here and untie me!"

The startled Mexican leaped from the saddle and came running up, staring in alarm at the trussed form of his chief. Then he whipped a knife from scabbard and cut the ropes to release Melrose.

"I just come from Mexitex—I was riding to tell Señor Everett that you were turned free from the *juzgado*," Fernandez informed the lawyer in Spanish. "Señor Everett is hiding in the cave."

Melrose reached out and helped himself to one of Fernandez's six-guns.

"*Bueno!*" whispered the lawyer. "Hap Kingman's sneaking up on Everett and the girl now. I reckon Anna's goin' to have the pleasure of seein' her hero punched full of bullet holes before many more minutes!"

28

DEATH IN THE RIO GRANDE

NO Mexican sentries lurked in the chaparral as Hap Kingman worked his way with infinite caution to the looming black mouth of the smuggler's den.

A faint glow of lantern light told the cowboy that someone was inside the cavern, and Hap knew that the probabilities were that this was the spot where the kidnapper brought Anna Siebert.

Removing his spurs so that their jingling chains would make no noise to betray him, the cowboy crept stealthily into the blackness of the cavern. His previous visits had familiarized him with the right-angle turn which the tunnel made, so that he did not have to grope his way along the rocky walls.

A moment later, to his straining eardrums, came the familiar voice of Everett Kingman, made guttural by too much whiskey:

"I'm givin' you till midnight, Anna. If Fernandez ain't back from Mexitex by then with the news that the sheriff turned Melrose loose,

I'm puttin' a bullet through you an' then I'm lightin' a shuck for Hermosillo."

Planting each boot sole carefully into the rubble underfoot, Hap Kingman rounded the turn of the subterranean passage.

Once more he was looking at the familiar underground chamber where he had once battled in showdown with Señor Giboso.

A lantern glowed on the crude pine table as before. Anna Siebert, tied with many turns of rope, was seated in a rickety chair by the table, a bandanna bound about her mouth.

The girl's eyes were staring at the spectacle of her captor seated on the table, flinging back his head in order to swill down a stiff jolt of rotgut whiskey.

"Reach for the roof, Everett!"

Hap Kingman shouted the command, even as he leaped into the circle of firelight, his twin six-guns leveled at his foster-brother.

With a hoarse bellow of surprise, the dissipated cowboy leaped off the table, hands swinging to his own low-thonged Colts.

"Hap!" squalled the half-breed spawn of Dev Hewett, his red-rimmed eyes slitting murderously. "How in hell—"

The outlaw broke off as he saw his foster-brother stalk forward behind jutting guns.

"Get your hands up, Everett, or I'll blast you wide open!" warned the cowboy. "I'm feelin' in a killin' mood, right now, and the gun I'm holdin' in my right hand belonged to the crooked owlhooter who sired you."

Everett Kingman still clutched the whiskey bottle in his right hand.

"You ain't takin' the girl!" screamed Everett, hauling back the hand that held the bottle. "Damn you, Hap—"

With all his force, the half-drunk cowboy hurled the brown glass bottle at Hap Kingman.

Anna Siebert's scream was muffled by her gag as she saw Hap try to dodge, saw his boots slip in the loose gravel underfoot. He flung up an arm, and the bottle struck a glancing blow across his head to shatter to bits in a spray of whiskey against the rock wall behind him.

Half stunned by the blow of the whiskey bottle, Hap Kingman sagged to his knees.

Dimly, through swimming vision, he saw the blurred figure of his foster-brother as Everett Kingman jerked his own six-guns from leather and brought them up, spitting lead.

Fighting against the dizziness which threatened to black out his senses, Hap Kingman tugged at his own guns.

The cavern was a nightmare of sound, as Everett Kingman rushed up with guns thundering madly.

With an effort that brought perspiration beading from his pores, Hap Kingman lifted the gun that was his misplaced six-gun legacy from Dev Hewett, and released the knurled hammer.

The sound of his shot blended with the burst of echoes from Everett's drunken and misaimed salvo, and the bullet sped through a milky wall of gunsmoke to halt Everett's berserk charge.

Knocked off his feet by the irresistible impact of a .45 missile tunneling the bridge of his nose, Everett Kingman was a dead man before his body slammed against the hard earth.

It was the first man Hap Kingman had ever slain, but there was no trace of regret in his heart as he got groggily to his feet and lurched across the cavern floor toward Anna Siebert.

Instead, he seemed to sense the dramatic retribution which Dev Hewett's six-gun had brought about against his own flesh and blood.

Holstering his Colt, Hap jerked off Anna Siebert's gag. Oblivious to her grasping word of thanks, the cowboy tore at the knots of her bonds with fingers that shook like ague.

"Let's get out of here, Anna," said the cowboy hoarsely, as the girl struggled up from the chair where she had spent hours as a despairing prisoner. "We'll leave Everett here. I don't owe him anything."

Avoiding the sprawled corpse of Everett Kingman, the two gripped hands and hurried toward the tunnel opening, the odor of burnt gunpowder sickening their nostrils.

The cool, moist smell of the Rio Grande greeted them as they rushed out of the cavern in the cliff's base and plowed through the whippy willows and cottonwood thickets to gain the muddy rim of the river.

Then, even as Hap Kingman turned with the intention of sweeping the girl into his embrace in thanksgiving at finding her alive, the cowboy froze.

Coming at him not a dozen paces away was Russ Melrose and the towering Mexican, Juan Fernandez.

Flinging the girl away from him, Hap dropped into a crouch and fired a single quick shot through the end of his holster.

The speedily aimed bullet caught Fernandez in the pit of the stomach, and it was only the Mexican's sidewise lurch that saved Kingman's life in the next instant.

The gun in Melrose's hand was leveling out for a point-blank shot, but Fernandez's toppling form tripped the lawyer's headlong rush and Melrose went down, sprawling in the mud.

Anna Siebert screamed as she saw Hap Kingman leap forward, kicking the smoking .45 out of the lawyer's grasp as Melrose struggled to regain his feet.

Then, as Melrose reared erect, the two men met in primitive hand-to-hand combat.

Locked in a grapple, they wrestled furiously

across the slippery brown mud on the river's edge.

With a strength born of desperation, Russ Melrose smashed out damaging blows which fought him clear of Kingman's grasp.

Disarmed and berserk with fear, the desperate lawyer raced out into the water, his slogging boots knocking sheets of muddy spray in all directions.

Anna Siebert froze in terror as she saw Hap Kingman disdain to use his own guns for a shot at the fleeing outlaw.

Instead, the cowboy lowered his jaw and raced out into the swirling water in hot pursuit.

Melrose turned, swinging a wild haymaker at Kingman.

But the cowboy ducked, and his shoulders slammed under Melrose's whizzing fist to knock the lawyer off his feet.

Rolling over and over as Kingman sought to throttle his foe, the two reared to their feet in a surge of foam and, standing in hip-deep water, squared off for their final desperate onslaught.

The current gripped them, and Hap Kingman felt Melrose's crushing grasp about his body as they went under the surface and were swept out in the deep channel of the river.

Grimly, Kingman kept his chin down to prevent Melrose's choking fingers from sinking home into his windpipe.

The tug of the current left them, as they settled down into the sludgy depths of the Rio Grande.

Hap's lungs were bursting for air, but he maintained his crushing grip on Melrose's threshing wrists as they struggled on the muddy river bottom.

Then Kingman felt the lawyer's struggles subside. A burst of bubbles tore from Melrose's straining lips, as river water surged into the outlaw's lungs.

Black oblivion threatened Kingman, as the bulk of the drowned lawyer threatened to pin him to the mud. Gasping river water into his lungs, the cowboy broke free of Melrose's entwining legs and lashed out for the surface.

He dragged life-giving air into his chest as the current swept him into the shallows.

Retching like a landed trout, Hap Kingman pulled his way to the bank, reached out to seize Anna Siebert's extended hand.

"Oh, Hap! Thank God—"

He held her close in the moonlight for a moment, as they both stared at the foam-padded surface of the Rio Grande. But the water-logged corpse of Russ Melrose remained in the depths.

With an impulsive gesture, the cowboy jerked Dev Hewett's cedar-butted .45 out of its mud-smeared holster.

With a grimace of mingled distaste and relief Hap Kingman threw the misplaced six-gun legacy out into the pool, saw it sink with a gurgling *chug* to join Russ Melrose on the bottom.

Then the cowboy turned back to the girl at his side and for a moment they stood there, each drinking in the full ecstasy of what they read in the other's eyes.

Kingman started to speak, but this was no moment for words. Anna Siebert moved closer into his arms and lifted her lips to meet those of the man she loved.

Center Point Large Print
600 Brooks Road / PO Box 1
Thorndike, ME 04986-0001 USA

(207) 568-3717

US & Canada:
1 800 929-9108
www.centerpointlargeprint.com